DEAD RAPUNZEL

VICTORIA HOUSTON

TYRUS
BOOKS

Published by
TYRUS BOOKS
an imprint of F+W Media, Inc.
10151 Carver Road, Suite 200
Blue Ash, OH 45242. U.S.A.
www.tyrusbooks.com

Hardcover ISBN 10: 1-4405-6849-9
Hardcover ISBN 13: 978-1-4405-6849-7
Paperback ISBN 10: 1-4405-6848-0
Paperback ISBN 13: 978-1-4405-6848-0
eISBN 10: 1-4405-6850-2
eISBN 13: 978-1-4405-6850-3

Printed in the United States of America.

10   9   8   7   6   5   4   3   2   1

Library of Congress Cataloging-in-Publication Data

Houston, Victoria,
   Dead Rapunzel / Victoria Houston.
     pages cm
   ISBN 978-1-4405-6848-0 (pb) -- ISBN 1-4405-6848-0 (pb) -- ISBN 978-1-4405-6849-7
(hc) -- ISBN 1-4405-6849-9 (hc) -- ISBN 978-1-4405-6850-3 (ebook) -- ISBN 1-4405-6850-2
(ebook)
   I. Title.
   PS3608.O88D4365 2015
   813'.6--dc23
                              2014046176

This is a work of fiction. Names, characters, corporations, institutions, organizations, events, or
locales in this novel are either the product of the author's imagination or, if real, used fictitiously.
The resemblance of any character to actual persons (living or dead) is entirely coincidental.

Many of the designations used by manufacturers and sellers to distinguish their products are
claimed as trademarks. Where those designations appear in this book and F+W Media, Inc. was
aware of a trademark claim, the designations have been printed with initial capital letters.

Cover design by Frank Rivera.
Cover image © David Fossler/123RF.

This book is available at quantity discounts for bulk purchases.
For information, please call 1-800-289-0963.

For Pete

"Three things in human life are important. The first is to be kind.
The second Is to be klnd. And the third is to be kind."

—HENRY JAMES

Chapter One

"Judith, you won't believe what I just bought! I made an offer of twenty-five million and it was accepted—the biggest deal I could ever hope to make in my *lifetime*. Oops, I better quiet down. I think I'm shouting into the phone."

Rudd Tomlinson took a quick look around, but with the exception of one couple sitting two tables away and an older man deep into his newspaper at the counter, the Grizzly Bear Café was empty. Early-morning regulars were long gone into the frigid out-doors where the icy March winds made people anxious to stay inside, turn up the furnace, and light the logs in the fireplace. While a few fanatic snowmobilers might venture into the coffee shop soon for an early lunch, it was the kind of day when a wise fisherman hunkered down to clean tackle.

Reassured she had not been overheard, Rudd lowered her voice as she said, "The people involved insisted I keep this a secret, so I haven't been able to say a word to anyone—not even you—but the deal is done. *Done*, believe it or not. I have just bought the largest collection of Georgia O'Keeffe art in private hands—two flower paintings, a sculpture, and a landscape.

"We finalize details on March eighteenth, and I will need you there as my witness. So, Judith, please, call me the moment you get this." Rudd couldn't help chuckling: "I can't believe I've been able to do this. We have to celebrate."

Setting the cell phone down on the table beside her mug of hot coffee, Rudd stared through the café picture windows at snow devils whirling down an ice-covered Main Street. A car crawled by, witness to the treacherous roadway.

In the distance she could hear the rumbling of a logging truck. With spring's road-weight limits just weeks away, the monster trucks were a constant sight as they barreled down Main Street, which was their only route south. The hundreds of lakes and rivers dotting the region made it impossible for the state highway to avoid meandering through the small town. Annoying as the fumes and noise might be for these few weeks in March and early April, Loon Lake residents rarely complained: Since the 1800s, timber had been the lifeblood of the Northwoods.

Rudd checked emails one last time before tucking the cell phone into a side pocket of her purse. She wondered if the silly, satisfied grin on her face made the couple at the nearby table think she was nuts. So what if they did. That eight A.M. phone call had made for an amazing morning.

Only Judith would appreciate what it meant to her. After all, who would have ever thought, twenty-two years ago when Michael and Ava were killed in that awful accident, that she would someday be one of the wealthiest people in northern Wisconsin? Not only rich but about to endow, design, and build one of the finest art museums in the Midwest.

Rudd paused, glancing down at her coffee cup. The happiness that had filled her heart moments ago faltered under the memory of losing her first husband and their only child so many, many years ago. To be perfectly honest, she thought as she drank the last of her third cup of coffee and handed her breakfast plate to the waitress, she would trade the money, the art, and every luxury in her life today—if she could have Michael and Ava back. She'd give it up in an instant. But that's easy to say when you know it isn't possible.

Getting to her feet, she reached around for her coat and started to pull it on. "Excuse me, but your coat is absolutely stunning," said the woman sitting with the man two tables away. "Is that a mink lining?"

Surprised at the comment and anxious to downplay the value of the coat that Philip had forced on her, Rudd offered an apologetic smile. "Yes, but it helps make the coat a little lighter to wear—you know how heavy sheepskin is. Warm but heavy."

Philip, the wealthy widower she had fallen in love with and married so unexpectedly five years earlier, had meant well when he insisted on buying her a fur coat. *Insisted* even though she said she did not want to wear anything so ostentatious. "You know I hate being over-accessorized," she had said. "It's not me, Philip. I don't care how much you love me." And so they had compromised on a custom-designed coat with shearling on the outside and the mink lining, which she was able to hide most of the time.

After wrapping a colorful wool scarf around her neck, Rudd pulled on a pair of fur-lined leather mitts, flung her purse over one shoulder, grabbed the flat leather case with all her notes inside, and pushed through the café door. The wind was so fierce against her face that she had to tuck her chin down into the scarf.

Hurrying to the curb where a path had been shoveled through the snow bank, Rudd stepped forward to peer past the parked cars for oncoming traffic. Another logging truck was thundering her way. She stepped back onto the curb, waiting for it to pass. Cold as it was, she felt more relaxed than she had in weeks.

Rudd loved her morning ritual, which she had fallen into after Philip's death. Seven days a week she would arrive early at the well-lit, warm little café where she would sit at the same table and order the same breakfast: a "green" omelet laced with fresh spinach and oozing goat cheese, one buttery brioche, a small OJ, and three cups (never more, never less) of black coffee. She made it a habit to arrive at seven-thirty so she could be on the curb by nine, ready to cross to the modest brick-and-stone building that she had purchased and was renovating into offices for the curatorial staff she hoped to hire soon. Speaking of which, she made a mental note to scan her notes—

Before she could finish that thought, she was airborne, pushed so hard that she flew off her feet. The logging truck came at her, crushing her beneath its massive tires.

Michael stood smiling. He was holding Ava, who was waving happily at her mom. Nothing appeared to have changed: Ava was her darling two-and-a-half-year-old self, Michael as handsome as the last time they had embraced. Ecstatic, Rudd ran toward them. She started to apologize for her coat only to realize she was wearing a T-shirt and shorts. That's right, she remembered, we're planning to take Ava out on the new pontoon and surprise her with that plastic fishing rod—the kiddie pole with a neon-green crappie hanging off the line. Michael had found it at the five-and-dime store. Fun!

Back in the café kitchen, eighteen-year-old Chip Dietz was starting to attack the morning's dirty dishes when he glanced through the window over the sink just as an elderly man, shoulders hunched into his parka, head bare, ran by—*running* even though he had a face that looked to be a hundred years old. Of course, Chip shrugged. With a wind chill of thirty below zero, who wouldn't run? He went back to sorting the dirty silverware.

A moment later he heard a scream of metal on metal. Oh no, I'll bet it's that old man, thought Chip. He slipped on the ice and fell in front of a car—bet you anything.

Chip rushed through the swinging kitchen doors and past the counter to the dining area. The morning waitress stood with her forehead pressed against the front window as he ran up.

"Call 911!" she shouted. Chip dove for the phone.

Chapter Two

"Good morning, Dani. Any luck yet?" asked Lewellyn Ferris, Chief of the Loon Lake Police, as she pulled out a chair and sat down to watch over the young intern's shoulder. "I know you've been here since seven this morning, which I appreciate."

Contrary to appearances—which included a six-inch eagle tattooed up her right forearm (the name "Herb" etched in scarlet below the talons), two silver rings piercing her left nostril, and vivid green-violet spikes exploding from the top of her head (all of which made her look more like a contestant on a goth reality show than a cop)—Dani Wright had an uncanny talent for demystifying computer code.

And she did wear the uniform of the Loon Lake Police with "Intern" embossed on the pocket over her right breast.

How Dani had come to be working alongside Loon Lake Police Chief Lewellyn Ferris was one of those crazy accidents of life. To earn money to pay for her cosmetology degree at the local tech college, Dani had taken a part-time job as an administrative assistant in the office of the local technical college president, a woman who was helpless when it came to using a computer, not to mention reading a spreadsheet.

Before long, the president knew whom to call every time she locked up "the damn mouse" or crashed her system. When the college website was hacked by a spammer siphoning money from students, and even the guys in the IT department were flummoxed, it was Dani who had worked the keyboard to locate the perpetrator.

For reasons no one could quite understand, the creative instinct and agile fingers that fueled Dani's interest in hair design played a similar role in solving complex computer puzzles, a talent with more lucrative potential than cosmetology. At least that's what Chief Ferris was able to convince her of, despite the siren song of the beauty salon.

"Dani," she had argued, "what if you didn't have to *work* in a salon when you didn't want to? What if after a few years working for the Loon Lake Police you could afford to *buy* a salon? Or two? Or seven? And do only the hair you want to do, the way you want to do it? What if?"

So it was that Dani had grinned and shrugged and agreed to come on board. She soon switched her major to law enforcement and started working part-time with the Loon Lake Police. Though she was only a lowly intern, she had proven to be one of the sharpest IT trackers in the upper Midwest.

The timing had been excellent, as cyber crime had been escalating in rural areas. Less than a month after Dani started her internship, two banks in Tomahawk were hacked. It took her less than a week to point the county sheriff in the direction of the hackers.

"Hey, yeah, good morning, Chief," said Dani, eyes locked on the monitor in front of her. "Nothing yet, but I feel like I'm getting close."

The computer, a laptop, belonged to Butch Johnson, owner of a small T-shirt and tattoo shop, who had been fleeced for more than a thousand bucks by some creep selling counterfeit Green Bay Packers jerseys online.

"Right before the Super Bowl, too, doncha know," Butch had said when he called in to report the theft. "Green Bay was playing and I had customers desperate for those jerseys. That's why I didn't take time to check the jabone out. My fault, I know, but is it too late to blow a whistle on the guy?"

"Of course not," said Lew. "You were victimized. I'll see what we can do. Come in Tuesday and bring your computer. We have an intern who is an IT expert. She may be able to help us locate the crook. Just don't drop that laptop before you get here."

"Don't you worry, Chief. Tell you what—if that gal can get me my money back she gets a free tattoo—her choice." Unfortunately he had made that promise when Dani was within earshot.

"Whoa, that's sweet," said Dani. "How soon can I start?"

Ouch, thought Lew. She could live with the spiky hair and the piercings. Were there many young people in Loon Lake without them? But another tattoo . . . Lew checked the Policy and Procedures manual, where it was explicitly stated that such an off-the-books arrangement was highly illegal. She was relieved, Dani disappointed.

"Well . . . Chief," she had argued, "I could get the tattoo where it can't be seen."

"You must be kidding," Lew had said with an appalled look on her face.

"Getting close, Chief," said Dani now, pausing her dancing fingers to sip from the cup of cold coffee next to the keyboard. "Once I locate the log file in Mr. Johnson's computer, we may have a digital trail, and once we have that—we can nail the sucker." Dani was cackling with satisfaction when the door to the conference room opened.

Marlaine, the morning dispatcher, poked her head in: "Chief Ferris, I just got a 911 alert that there's been a bad accident down on Main Street—right in front of the Grizzly Bear Café. A pedestrian may have been killed."

"Uh-oh," said Lew, pushing back her chair, "I knew the day was going too well. Marlaine, Officer Roger Adamczak is on duty this morning. Will you please call him and tell him to meet me there? I'll need the coroner, too. Pecore's wife will answer, so try to find out if he's still sober. It is before noon, isn't it?"

"I know the drill," said Marlaine.

Following the dispatcher out the door, Lew paused. "Dani—you get anything, call my cell ASAP, and don't say a word to Butch until you talk to me."

"Will do, Chief."

Osborne was slipping the last tax document into a manila folder when the cordless phone in his kitchen rang. He checked caller ID before picking up. This was one morning when he would rather talk to his accountant than listen to some politician plaguing the line with "robo" calls. But the name on his phone was familiar.

"Mallory," he said, "if it's not critical can I call you back? I have a ten-thirty appointment with my accountant—"

"Sure, Dad," said his oldest daughter. "We can catch up later. Just wanted to let you know I've taken a new job up north and hope you don't mind that I'm moving in with you until I get my own place. So, my old room, okay?" And she hung up.

Osborne looked down at the phone in his hand, stunned. *Mallory moving home?*

That changes my life, he thought. And just when he and Lew had settled into a cozy rhythm of spending nights at one another's homes. Hmm. He loved his daughter, but . . .

As he drove into town, Osborne puzzled over Mallory's news. How on earth could any company in the Northwoods (sometimes referred to by people from the cities as "the backwoods") of Wisconsin possibly pay his daughter the kind of money she was making as a senior vice president for a Chicago marketing firm? Could there be a man involved? Divorced over a year now, his daughter had lonely moments, he knew.

As he neared the intersection by the hospital, Osborne's cell phone rang. "Doc?" It was Lew, sounding peeved. "Pecore and his wife decided to take a spring break early and he forgot to leave word, of course. They're in Fort Myers with their daughter, who just had a baby, and I have a poor soul who has just been flattened by a logging truck in the middle of town. How soon can you get here?"

"A fatality?"

"Let's just say injuries too severe to survive. Hope you haven't just eaten."

"I'll swing back to the house for my instrument bag and see you shortly."

After executing a U-turn, Osborne called the accountant's office to apologize for cancelling at the last minute. "I'm sorry," he said, "but I just got a call from Chief Ferris, who needs me to help with a fatal traffic accident. I'll drop off the documents and call later to reschedule, if that's all right."

"Certainly, Dr. Osborne. Dennis will understand," said the secretary.

Osborne knew he would. Dennis, like many of his fishing buddies who had not yet retired, envied Osborne a lifestyle where every day could be a great day for fishing. They were also impressed that his interest in forensic dentistry had opened the door to helping the Loon Lake Police as a deputy coroner whenever Pecore was indisposed, which was often given Pecore's favorite pastime: being over-served.

But they were more impressed with Osborne's familiarity with the chief of the Loon Lake Police. At least he hoped they didn't know everything.

Chapter Three

Osborne pulled into the parking lot beside the Grizzly Bear Café. An ambulance and two police cars were blocking the street. Grabbing his instrument bag, he hurried over to where Lew was huddled on the curb in front of the café entrance. Even in her heavy winter parka, lined deerskin mitts, and insulated boots, she looked cold.

"This won't be easy, Doc," was all Lew said, pointing ahead and to the left, her breath a cloud in the bitter air. Osborne looked in the direction she was pointing, then away. He caught the eye of an EMT waiting nearby, who nodded in understanding. What was left of the individual who had been hit was difficult for even the most experienced of first responders to stomach.

"Do we have any identification of this . . . woman?" asked Osborne. The wheels of the truck had crushed the head, masking any identifying features. Not even the jaw remained intact and Osborne was sure a dental ID might be difficult if not impossible.

It was the clothing—a shearling coat, a bright blue scarf, traces of a wool sweater, and burgundy fleece leggings on the only extremities not damaged—that made it obvious the victim was female.

"The only positive news, at least for our work, is that on impact the victim's purse flew a good forty feet into the snow bank up a ways, so we have her driver's license," said Lew, "and her cell phone.

"Name is Rudd Tomlinson. One of the waitresses knows her. Said she had breakfast at the Grizzly Bear Café every morning—

same time, seven days a week. Said she was married to the late Philip Tomlinson. I'm not familiar with anyone named Tomlinson, so I'm not sure whom to notify, but I'll get started on it as soon as you finish, Doc. Then the EMTs can move the remains to the morgue."

She turned away and lowered her voice. "The driver of the logging truck is in bad shape. I had Roger take him into the café to stay warm and get some fluids in him before he goes into shock."

"Poor guy," said Osborne. "I can't imagine how he must feel. Not sure how helpful this will be, Lew, but I knew Philip and his first wife. I was not aware he had remarried. He died about two years ago, and I know that only because it was in the alumni newsletter that I get from Campion, the Catholic boarding school where we both went. Philip was at least five years ahead of me. He was not a young man when he passed away, so his children must be in their thirties."

"Do you know whom we should notify?" asked Lew. "Children, other relatives?"

"Not sure," said Osborne. "I do know that Philip and Caroline were summer residents for many years. They had a family compound up on Thunder Lake, just this side of the boundary between Loon Lake Township and Newbold. Generations ago the Tomlinson family made a fortune in barbed wire."

"I appreciate the history, Doc, but I need names and phone numbers. I've made a quick search of her wallet, which I found in the purse, but there's nothing in it except charge cards and cash. I need next of kin."

"I realize that," said Osborne, closing his eyes to think. "Bear with me. I'm trying my best to remember . . . Okay, I treated one of the Tomlinson daughters for a broken tooth and she had an unusual name like Sybil or Sinclair or . . . Look, I'm sure I have the family records at home, so I can check for those as soon as we are finished here."

"That may be the best we can do for the moment, but it will help," said Lew. "One more reason to be nice to you." She touched him lightly with her left elbow, so lightly no one else observing the scene of the accident would have noticed but enough that Osborne's day brightened in spite of the grim business ahead.

"If it's okay with you, Chief Ferris," he said, stepping into his role as deputy coroner and talking loudly enough for the half dozen bystanders to hear, "I'll take that driver's license and initiate completing the death certificate so the body can be moved. Damn cold standing out here."

Looking down at the information on the driver's license for the victim, Osborne was surprised to see how young she was: only forty-seven? Maybe he was wrong about Philip Tomlinson. If he were still alive, that guy would have been in his late sixties. Could it be that she was married to a Philip, Jr.?

As he recorded the details that an insurance company would need—location, estimated time of death—he could feel his fingers freezing in the stiff wind. He would leave it for a pathologist to make an official confirmation of the cause of death, which would be attached to the police report of the accident. Given the weather, he was thankful that the condition of the victim required only a visual exam.

Minutes later he was able to join Lew and Roger in the warmth of the Grizzly Bear Café. Roger Adamczak was the older of Lew's two full-time Loon Lake Police officers and not a man given to subtle observations.

A struggling insurance salesman, Roger had been in his early forties when he decided law enforcement was the way to simplify his life. He made the mistake of assuming the toughest duty in a tiny town like Loon Lake might be writing tickets for expired parking meters: a no-stress guarantee of a nice pension.

Then Lewellyn Ferris was promoted to chief and Roger got assigned to patrolling for drunk drivers. Too often the drunken motorists were former clients who did not appreciate Roger's new role: raising instead of lowering their insurance premiums.

But once an insurance salesman, always one. Whenever there was an accident—whether traffic, construction, or boating—Roger could be heard expounding on liability issues, which was what he was doing as Osborne walked up to the café counter. Like an excited grouse eager to attract the ladies, the officer had fluffed his feathers and was making loud noises.

"Ah baloney, that driver is lying," said Roger, his voice easy to hear throughout the small café. "He's just saying that to avoid the logging company getting sued, Chief. Jeez, his family probably owns the operation, y'know. He's got to—this could mean a million-dollar lawsuit. And it'll take years to settle. You just watch."

"Roger's questioning the driver's story," said Lew with one eyebrow up. Having inherited Roger from her late predecessor, it was only because she had a good heart and knew how critical the pension was to him that she hadn't booted him from the force years earlier.

She held a finger to her lips as a man emerged from the restroom and approached them. The driver was in his late twenties and wearing soiled, rust-colored Carhartt overalls under a beat-up, olive-green parka, with bulky driving gloves jammed into ripped pockets. His color was ashen, and Osborne could see his hands trembling.

"Bob, would you please tell Dr. Osborne what you saw this morning—before the accident. He's our deputy coroner and will need your information to complete the death certificate."

Osborne got the message: Lew wanted his take on what the young man would say. Previous collaborations had taught them that each listened to people with a different ear. Osborne's years of practicing dentistry had trained him to listen for hints that a patient's problems might originate somewhere other than their teeth. Lew listened with a woman's intuition: a knack for recognizing the emotions underlying statements—or withheld to hide a truth.

When they compared what each had heard—or thought they'd heard—the results could be startling.

"Of course," said the driver, his body sagging into a chair at a nearby table. He ran his fingers through his hair and heaved a sigh as he said, "Dr. Osborne, I'm Robert Sittell but I go by 'Bob.' I've been driving for my father's logging operation for ten years. Never had anything like this happen before. Never. We have our vehicles inspected annually, brakes are good—"

His voice shook as badly as his hands. "I was coming down Main Street here, just like yesterday. Not going too fast 'cause it's icy, w-a-a-y icy out there. I saw the woman standing on the curb just fine, y'know. Fact is, she's been standing there every morning these past few weeks. I come through on the way to Wausau five days a week.

"So this morning I'm like almost to her when this old guy comes from behind the building—on the south side by the drive-way—and pushes her out in front of me. No way I could stop. Well, I *could've* hit the brakes, but I'd still never have been able to stop without hitting her. You know how long it takes to stop one of these mothers?"

He gestured toward the front windows at the truck, which was now parked nearly half a block down from where he had hit the woman. "I pulled over as soon as I could without jackknifing and taking out the whole goddamn block."

"You saw someone push her?" asked Osborne.

"I swear." Off to one side, Roger gave a disbelieving shrug.

"Officer?" A teenage boy wearing an apron who had been standing behind the café counter, listening to the driver's story, raised a hand so Lew could see he wanted to say something.

"Yes?" she asked, turning toward him.

"He's right. I saw an old man running in that direction right before the accident. Saw him out the window here. When I heard that truck's brakes, I was sure it was the old guy got hit."

Lew sat quietly for a long moment. She turned to Osborne. "Doc, go stop the EMTs, would you please? Tell them no moving the body yet. Roger, you call the highway department. I want the road closed two blocks in both directions. They'll have to reroute the traffic." She punched a number into her cell phone.

"Marlaine, please call Officer Donovan and tell him I'm sorry but he'll have to come in now. We have a crime scene to work."

Chapter Four

Lew was savoring a final sip of hot coffee when her pager buzzed. She reached for her walkie-talkie. "Yes?"

"Chief, Officer Donovan just arrived. Okay for me to head out now?"

Sitting beside Lew at the café counter, Osborne could hear the anxiety in Roger's voice and he sympathized. Tasked with keeping cars away from the four-block stretch that Lew wanted cordoned off, Roger had to be freezing: Roadblocks do not come with space heaters.

"If the DOT boys have the 'detour' signs up, you're free to go, Roger. But before you do that, ask Todd to meet me here in the café, would you please? And thanks for putting in the extra time this morning."

A grudging "yep" could be heard.

Within minutes, Todd Donovan, thirty years Roger's junior and a dedicated marathon runner, appeared in the doorway of the café. In spite of his youth and health, and even though the walk to the café was only a block from where he had parked his squad car, the officer's cheeks were bright red above his buttoned-up parka. Lew beckoned for him to pull over a chair. "Need something warm to drink?" Todd nodded with appreciation as a cup of hot coffee appeared.

After Lew had filled him in on the status of the victim and the truck driver's allegation that the woman had been pushed, Todd asked, "And you believe him?"

"I do," said Lew. "The look in his eye, I believe him."

Todd glanced over at Osborne, who said, "I do, too."

"So I've been thinking," said Lew, tapping her pen on the counter. "The snow and ice and the freezing temps make this not the easiest crime scene to work. So we'll have to do the best we can. We'll follow the usual protocols, but when it comes to photos, it is so cold that our cameras may not work very well. For one thing, the tracks left by the truck's tires after the driver started to brake indicate he didn't see her until the last minute. We need to document those, but I'm worried.

"Hate to shoot the scene and find everything blurry, which is what happened two weeks ago when I tried to take shots of an eagle that someone had poisoned. I thought I would ask Ray Pradt to help out with the photography. He's shot winter scenes for his calendars, so he must have equipment that will work in cold weather—"

"Not only that, Chief," said Todd. "We have our cameras in our warm cars. I think it's the temperature difference when it's this cold that affects the lens. I'll bet you anything Ray keeps his gear in that old pickup of his. And if that beater has heat, I owe you money."

"You're right," said Lew. She turned to Osborne. "Doc, can you try to reach Ray? He can't be ice fishing on a day this cold. Tell him I need black-and-white as well as color. With all this snow, the black-and-white might pick up shadows. Tell him I want shots of the roadway as well as the street in both directions: the buildings, the sidewalks, cars parked nearby. If anyone walks by while he's shooting, I want photos of them, too. This is hardly tourist season, so it will be good to know who's crazy enough to be out and about when it's this cold—and why."

"Another thing, Chief," said Todd. "Checking the weather this morning, it's going to warm up. If we have a melt, any evidence left in the snow, the tire tracks, any tracks left by the individual who pushed the victim, are likely to disappear."

"Good point," said Lew. "Damn, it's so overcast now and it'll be pitch black by five. Whew—talk about a short window. Not sure if tracking will be of any value, but let's start with the driveway. That's where the kid saw the old guy running before the victim was pushed."

"What direction did he go?" asked Todd. "If we know that—"

"We don't. All we have is the driver insisting he saw a man push the victim before he hit her. His focus was on trying to stop his vehicle and avoid a further catastrophe."

"Look, Lew," said Osborne, aware of her frustration, "I'll take care of reaching Ray. I'll tell him you need the photos and possible help with tracking if you and Todd come across anything. Does that sound right?"

"It's a start," said Lew. "Doc, you can help by going through that woman's purse one more time. I have to reach her next of kin, and no luck with that cell phone. I have Dani getting in touch with the provider in hopes they'll give us the code. Until then the phone is locked. While I found the wallet with the license and credit cards, I haven't had time to go through the rest of the stuff in that bag.

"Looks like there's a lot in there, too. Makeup, medications, who knows what else. If you would go through it and make a list of the contents, that would help. If you don't find any more personal information, let me know. I may have to ask you to drive out to the address on the driver's license and see if we can reach someone at the home or a neighbor—"

"I'll take care of it, Lew."

After Lew and Todd left the café, Osborne poured one more cup of coffee and settled in with his assignments. Any time spent in the warmth of the little café was fine with him. First on his list was to reach his neighbor. He punched Ray's cell number into his phone and waited.

When Ray didn't answer, Osborne waited for his voicemail, wondering what he would hear this time, since Ray had a habit of recycling messages ranging from the insightful ("This is Ray Pradt hoping you 'fish like it matters'—and leave me your number") to the profane (a riff on "wedding tackle" that Osborne had learned to cut off before the ribald punch line). He wondered if Ray's voicemail messages would have been different if the guy had been a responsible husband and father instead of a not-bad-looking, unattached fishing guide living in a trailer home painted to look like a fearsome fish.

This morning the voicemail was one of Ray's birdcalls—the trill of a spring robin (highly inappropriate in Osborne's opinion, given that any bird outdoors would be a frozen specimen)— followed by "Yep, it's thirty below and falling. This is Ray—leave your name and number. Will return from the Caribbean one of these days."

"Ray," said Osborne, "I know you're there and I need to talk to you ASAP. Lew's got trouble—" Before he could finish, his phone buzzed with Ray calling back.

"Got it. Be there in fifteen," said Ray after Osborne had filled him in on the situation. "Tell Chief Ferris not to worry. Both my cameras work fine in weather this cold. Chances are I'll have photos for her to review this evening—got everything digital now, y'know.

"By the way, you say it was old man Tomlinson's wife who was run over? I guided that guy a couple times back about ten years ago—Phil and a couple of his buddies. As I drive over, I'll see if I can try to remember who else was there."

After entering as much information on the death certificate as could be done with the information available, Osborne reached for the victim's purse, which Lew had left on the table beside him.

It was the type of bag that his daughters carried: roomy, with straps long enough to be slung over the shoulder. The black leather was of good quality and the interior held several zippered compartments. Opening the purse, he could not help feeling guilty. Years of living with his late wife and raising two daughters had drilled into him the horror of violating the privacy of a woman's purse. Today was different: He had to hope the purse held secrets.

Osborne settled the bag on his lap and pulled it open so he could see the interior. He pulled out a red mesh envelope holding a compact, a tube of lipstick, and one ChapStick. Also in the bag were two pens and a small comb. Loose in the purse were a hairbrush with a colorful cloth cover, a small flashlight, two packets of Kleenex (one opened), a case with sunglasses, and another case with what looked to be reading glasses.

A zippered side pocket yielded a checkbook, a set of car keys, and a black leather card case. Cards that had been slipped into both sides of the small case included ones for a dry cleaner, a lawyer, a shoe-repair service, a building contractor, and three different individuals who appeared to be academics—one at Marquette University, another at Northwestern, and one at Yale.

The last card belonged to an art dealer from Venezuela. Then, folded tightly and tucked behind the art dealer's card was a slip of paper on which was written in longhand the following:

"In case of an emergency, my primary physician is Dr. Jerome Grant at Marshfield Clinic. My oncologist is Dr. Fred Waring at Marshfield Clinic. My emergency contact is Judith Fordham . . . " A cell phone number was included, as were phone numbers for each of the physicians.

To be sure he hadn't missed anything, Osborne reached back inside the zippered side pocket. Crunched into folds at the bottom was another piece of paper. Unfolded and smoothed out, it was a full-page listing of passwords for different devices and websites. At the bottom, as if it had been recently added, was the code for an iPhone.

Osborne reached for his own cell phone to call Lew. "Lew, I think I found the code to unlock the cell phone. Also the name of an emergency contact—do you want me to call that number?"

Lew didn't hesitate. "Yesterday."

Chapter Five

"Hello. Who is this?" asked a woman's voice.

"This is Dr. Paul Osborne in Loon Lake, Wisconsin. Am I speaking with Judith Fordham?"

"Yes. Why? How did you get this number?" The voice held an edge. Osborne hoped the call wouldn't be dropped before he could explain himself.

"I'm calling regarding Rudd Tomlinson—"

"Oh," said the woman, "I'm sorry. I thought you were someone asking for a donation. Let Rudd know I'm almost there. Maybe twenty miles away. But the roads are not great, so I'm taking my time. Please tell her I should be there before lunch and sorry I couldn't return her call. I tried, but sketchy service out here—kept dropping me."

"I . . . um . . . " Osborne wasn't sure where to start.

"Did you say your name is Osborne? You must be the new marketing director, but I thought we weren't meeting until next week. I am sorry to be running so late—it's the ice on these roads! Please tell Rudd she can start without me. A-a-n-d I can't *wait* to hear more about her amazing purchase."

"That's . . . ah . . . why I'm calling," said Osborne, surprised to feel pressure against the inside of his eyelids. "Your friend is dead. She was hit by a truck this morning."

Silence on the phone. A long, long pause. "Say that again?" No edge in her voice—only the quiet that comes with disbelief.

"I'm Dr. Paul Osborne—acting Loon Lake coroner. Our chief of police, Lewellyn Ferris, asked me to call you. We found a note in the victim's purse listing you as the person to be notified in case of an emergency. So I'm sorry to be calling with bad news. Are you Rudd Tomlinson's next of kin?"

"No, I'm not. I'm her friend—the one she counts on."

"Can you help us reach her next of kin?"

"Yes, of course. But can that wait until I get there? I'm her closest friend and I know the family well. They are not very nice people, and Rudd would want me to be the one to deliver the good news."

Osborne stared down at his phone: This was an odd conversation. "So you do know how to reach them?"

"Unfortunately." The edge was back, though Osborne didn't feel it directed at him. "Did you say this was an accident?"

"Not sure. The driver of the vehicle involved—a large logging truck—said that he saw someone push Mrs. Tomlinson. Now, I probably shouldn't be telling you that because it hasn't been confirmed, so please don't say anything—"

"Don't worry. I won't." And Osborne knew she wouldn't. Judith Fordham was blunt if not a touch cynical. She had an officious way to her. "Pushed, huh?"

"That's what the truck driver said. Chief Ferris has no one in custody—just a witness who may have seen a person in the vicinity and the truck driver. Hopefully, we'll know more when you get here. With the roads so bad I'm not sure we should be talking."

"Sure, I'll get off the phone, but one more question . . . " A long pause; then, "Do you think my friend knew what hit her?" The edge had given way to sadness.

"I—based on my initial exam, I am sure she died instantly." He didn't add the obvious, that the question ultimately was unanswerable.

"Hmm. Well . . . Rudd might be okay with that. Look, Dr. Osborne, I should make it into town within fifteen or twenty minutes. Has Rudd . . . Has her body been moved?"

"Not yet."

"Please tell whoever is in charge not to move her until I get there." And with that, the woman's voice broke. "Sorry, I have to pull over. I—"

"Take your time," said Osborne. "I'll give you directions. I'm afraid you'll have to park at the top of Main Street, as it's been blocked off until the police and EMTs are finished."

The woman who walked into the café half an hour later had composed herself. She was bundled into a long, black, quilted coat, with a bright red scarf muffling her chin and earmuffs of black fur covering her straight brown hair. The skin around her eyes was blotched, but she was not crying.

Undoing the scarf, she shook Osborne's hand and then hurried over to the picture window at the front of the café. She leaned forward, her gaze intent on the figure lying in the middle of the street. "How much longer will they keep her out there? It is so cold!" She was still speaking when Lew walked in the café door. Osborne pointed toward the woman standing at the window.

"Judith Fordham, I'm Lewellyn Ferris, Chief of the Loon Lake Police and in charge of this investigation," said Lew, pulling a glove off her right hand as she extended it. "I am so sorry about your friend. And I'm sorry Officer Donovan wouldn't let you near her body, but the circumstances right now are complex. We've been told she may have been pushed in front of the truck that hit her."

Judith's eyes went black as she said in a deliberate tone, "I am not surprised. Rudd recently inherited a great deal of money under circumstances that upset a number of people. And we all know what *that* can do."

"Dr. Osborne said you know how to reach her next of kin?"

"Yes, I have been Rudd Tomlinson's closest friend for twenty years and I know how to reach the family, but by that I mean her late husband's adult children. Rudd herself has no living relatives. If it is okay with you, Chief Ferris, I think I would rather call them a little later when I have some privacy and I can reach them on a landline phone—my cell phone isn't working great up here."

"Certainly, but in the meantime there are some legalities that have to be handled. Whom do I contact?"

"That's me. I am the executor of her will, which is how I know that I am her legal heir, and *that*, for the record, will come as a surprise to the Tomlinson crowd." She gave a grim smile. "Will her body be out in the cold like that much longer?"

"No. I'm about to let the EMTs move her. We needed photos in order to document what may be a crime scene, but I believe the photographer has finished his work around the victim."

Looking through the window, Osborne could see Ray working on the far side of the street. He had set up a tripod and appeared to be adjusting his camera to shoot along the sidewalk and the snow bank. "I've asked him to shoot the entire two-block radius," said Lew. "He'll be here for a while. In the meantime, I hope you don't mind coming with us to the victim's home. I want no one on that property until we have been able to conduct a full search of the premises."

"Certainly, but may I see my friend before she's moved?"

Lew paused. "Are you sure you want to do that? I'm afraid those truck tires did a great deal of damage . . . "

"I know," said Judith, backing away toward the door. Tears glistened in her eyes. "I know, but I need to say goodbye."

"Of course. I'll signal for the EMTs to stand back. Take your time, but, please, don't touch the body. I doubt there is evidence of who pushed her, but we can't risk contaminating—"

"I understand, but—could I just leave her with something of mine? So she isn't alone . . . " Judith's voice caught in a sob.

"Yes, we'll document whatever it is that you leave with her. It's okay." Lew gave her arm a reassuring pat.

Osborne walked over to stand beside Lew. They watched in the grey wintery light as Judith walked past the ambulance where the EMTs were slapping their shoulders to stay warm. Curious bystanders had been coming and going.

One of the waitresses, who had heard both the truck driver's allegation and the fact that Chip Dietz had seen a person who might have pushed the victim, had been telling customers and calling friends. The gossip that a murder may have occurred was spreading fast, drawing more people to the scene.

"I hope she does this quickly. I really don't want to have to deal with a television crew this morning," said Lew, muttering under her breath to Osborne.

Judith knelt beside the body of her friend. Slipping her red scarf from around her neck, Judith folded it twice before laying it gently over what had been Rudd's face. Then she stood and watched as the EMTs prepared the body before slipping the still form into the body bag.

Osborne and Lew walked out to join her as she watched. Before the bag was zipped closed, Judith said to one of the EMTs, "Can you be sure my scarf is covering her face inside that . . . " She didn't finish her sentence, but turned to Lew and Osborne as the bag was loaded into the ambulance. "Seems silly, I know, but I want to keep her warm."

Chapter Six

Skeletons hovered over the road as Osborne followed Lew's cruiser down the county highway that wound through a hardwood forest. Stands of birch and maple and aspen stood naked under the grey sky, stripped of their summer glory. As Osborne's Subaru crested a hill, the hardwoods gave way to evergreens—feathered branches of pine and spruce so heavy with snow, their bony arms scraped his windshield as if warning him away.

Plows and sanding trucks appeared to have forgotten this remote stretch of the highway. Ice hidden beneath furrows of a recent snowfall forced Osborne to drive so slowly that he lost sight of Lew's cruiser as she followed Judith's SUV. He trusted that brake lights would alert him when it was time to turn off the county road.

"Don't rely on your GPS, you two. Better follow me or you're likely to end up at one of the family places instead of the main house, which is Rudd's home," Judith had insisted when they started out.

Two miles further and Osborne relaxed at the sight of winking brake lights. After turning down Tomlinson Road, the three cars came to a stop in front of a tall, wrought-iron gate guarding the entrance to a private drive while Tomlinson Road continued on. Judith got out of her car and trudged through newly fallen snow to a small metal box mounted on a stanchion to the left of the locked gate. She lifted the cover and punched in a code. The gate swung open to a recently plowed driveway that had been well sanded.

The private drive wove through more evergreens before reaching an open field, a sea of snow sculpted by wind into waves of silvery meringue. The drive ended in a clearing alongside two wings of black timber, with Thunder Lake in the background. The wings, which reached for the sky, framed a twenty-foot wall of glass banded with steel.

"Wow," said Lew, gesturing toward the house as Judith walked up. "Did this arrive from another planet?"

Judith managed a smile. "Isn't it something? It was finished just before Philip died. Rudd was so happy he was able to enjoy it even for a short time." While she spoke, she reached into her purse and pulled out a small remote. One click and the glass wall split in two, each panel sliding silently into the wings.

"Certainly not a hunting shack," said Osborne, trying to imagine how much the timbered wings must have cost—dark wood like that wasn't native to northern Wisconsin.

He glanced around. "Where is the old Tomlinson lodge? Moved to another section of the property?"

"I remember fishing this lake with my father when I was a kid and the lodge was quite the place, with walls made of logs three feet in diameter and a massive river-rock chimney. Had to have been built in the late eighteen hundreds from virgin timber. You know, you don't see lodges like that any longer."

As he spoke, they followed Judith across a heated walkway that led into the glass-enclosed, two-story foyer. "That old place had seen better days by the time Rudd met Philip," said Judith. "There were structural issues, including the chimney, that were not solvable. So Philip had the lodge torn down, but they saved the wood from the walls and floors for use in the museum. Of course, a couple of his kids are convinced Rudd was behind tearing down the old place—they hate her for that."

"I'm sorry, but what did you just say—they are saving the wood for *what*?" asked Osborne as they paused a few feet from a door of the same dark wood as the wings.

Before Judith could answer, the door opened and a dark-haired woman in a fur coat, unaware they were standing there, backed her way into the room. One arm clutched a large purse slung over one shoulder while the other arm encircled a flat object wrapped in a pillowcase. She turned around and jerked back, startled.

"Judith! What are *you* doing here?"

"Excuse me, Sloane. The question is what are *you* doing here? And what's that under your arm?" Judith's tone was not friendly. Osborne threw a worried glance at Lew.

"Oh, just a little thing of Dad's. Nothing special. And who the hell are these people? Rudd didn't say she's expecting visitors."

Stepping in front of Judith, Lew said, "I'm Lewellyn Ferris, Chief of the Loon Lake Police, and my deputy and I are here to secure the premises as part of a criminal investigation. No one will be allowed to enter the home or remove anything until we have completed our investigation."

"I—I—this in inexcusable. What are you talking about? Philip Tomlinson was my father. I have every right to be here whenever—"

Osborne watched the woman's face as she spoke. She wore the makeup of a woman spending too much money on a fruitless attempt to look better. The wrinkles of age do not cooperate with even the most expensive of cosmetics, and everything about this woman looked expensive: the fur coat, the fur boots, and the multiple rings on her fingers. Years of bending over faces in the dental chair had made Osborne sensitive to the perils of makeup on women (and some men) as they age. When the effect was as bad as it was on Sloane, he considered it an act of desperation.

Like a muskie fisherman with a lunker on the line, he couldn't help being interested in how this scenario would play out. Sloane, however confident she might have been in her attempt to sneak something out of her stepmother's home, had two formidable foes: Lew had the authority of the law while Judith was angered by the attempted theft, which she was not hesitant to block.

"Sloane," said Judith, her voice even, "I don't think you are aware that Rudd was killed in a traffic accident this morning. I'm sorry you have to hear it this way, but I hope that explains why Chief Ferris and Dr. Osborne are here.

"Thing is, her death may not have been an accident. The driver of the truck that hit her has sworn that he saw someone—a man—push her. If that's true, she was murdered, and that's why this house will be off-limits to everyone, including myself." Judith turned to Lew. "Chief Ferris, maybe you can explain what has to happen here."

"Until we know more about your stepmother's death," said Lew, "this house and its contents may be critical to our criminal investigation. We'll be searching the interior and any outer buildings for evidence or indications of why Mrs. Tomlinson was killed. So please tell me your name and why you happen to be here at this time—and I will appreciate it if you would please set down whatever that is that you're carrying."

Grief hits people in different ways, but Osborne had never seen it expressed in quite this way: Before she could hide it, a smile of sly satisfaction flashed across Sloane's face.

"I see," she said, backing away. "But Judith, if Rudd is dead—then all this," she turned toward the open door behind her, "all this belongs to the family now—me, Tim, Kenzie . . ."

"Sloane," said Judith, "Chief Ferris just asked you to put down whatever that is you are holding. Please do so. The house is not yours, and in the meantime, I have Rudd Tomlinson's power of attorney and I give consent to the search of this house."

Sloane stared at Judith and did not move. She was a heavy-faced woman who might have been attractive before appetite and attitude marred whatever vestiges of kindness or class possibly existed. With a sneer she said, "Alrighty then," and dropped the object onto the floor. "It's going to be mine someday anyway."

"I'm afraid not."

"And just what do you mean by that?" asked the woman as she stepped forward, shoving her face in front of Judith's. Judith did not back up.

"Six months ago Rudd established a trust to support the new museum. All her assets belong to the trust, and I am the administrator of the trust."

This time the woman had nothing to say. Osborne watched as anger mixed with fear contorted her features. Throwing her head back, she set her shoulders and turned toward the glass doors. With a wave of her hand, the doors slid open.

"Judith Fordham, I am calling our lawyer. You won't get away with this." She stomped out and disappeared to the left of the entrance.

"Wait—I want to talk to you," said Lew, rushing toward Sloane as the doors slid closed behind her.

"She's not going far," said Judith, sounding disgusted. "She has a McCottage a short walk down the road. You won't have any trouble finding her. Chief Ferris, I don't know what you think, but I find it very interesting that she was in here. The timing, you know?"

Judith reached down to pick up the object that Sloane had dropped onto the floor. She pulled off the pillowcase to expose a small oil painting. "It's *The Bay of Naples with the Castel dell'Ovo*, a painting by Corot, who was an artist Rudd loved. The original was her wedding gift from Philip. Worth about two million dollars."

"Are you saying that Sloane was planning to walk out of here with a painting worth millions?" asked Lew.

"She thought she was," said Judith with a tight smile. "You'll find that Philip's children—all three of them—haven't grasped the reality that they are not Philip Tomlinson's heirs. They are not as entitled as they believe.

"Not to worry," she said in response to the concern on Lew's face. "This painting is a replica. But Sloane doesn't know that."

Judith lowered her head, raised her eyebrows, and said with grim satisfaction, "Rudd was very aware of what Sloane and her brother were up to. Between the two of us, Rudd and myself, we've made sure Sloane and Tim have a closet full of reproductions. The originals are safe in a temperature-controlled storage facility in Minneapolis, which was designed for the storage of fine art and antiques. They'll be furious when they find out."

Chapter Seven

"Chief Ferris, if you don't mind, I'm going to take over the sitting area on the upstairs balcony for a few minutes," said Judith. "I get better cell reception up there, and I really need to get those calls in to Rudd's other stepchildren—Tim and his younger sister, Kenzie."

Now that she had her coat, scarf, and hat off Osborne could see that Judith was a pleasant-faced woman. She might not have been pretty, but her face was open and her brown eyes frank. A slight hook to her nose reminded him of a Roman statue. The patrician look suited her well-spoken manner.

As she spoke of the need to make the calls, her shoulders had slumped. Osborne recognized that overwhelming kick in the gut that comes with the loss of someone close to you. As self-contained as she had been when they'd entered Rudd's home, the fact was only hours had passed since her friend's death. Over the next days, weeks, and months, Judith would learn that grief has a way of sneaking up on you.

"Take all the time you need," said Lew as she slipped off her parka and set it on a nearby chair. "But, here, first slip on these nitrile gloves and try not to touch anything, not even the hand-rails on the stairway." She handed Judith a pair of gloves from the box she carried in the cruiser.

"Also, I'll need you to be careful where you walk. Follow Dr. Osborne and myself so we don't contaminate more of the area than is necessary."

"May I tell the family everything? What the truck driver said? That he saw Rudd pushed?"

"Yes," said Lew, "that will explain why law enforcement has to treat their stepmother's death as a crime—and why no one is allowed in her home until it has been thoroughly searched."

"I'll make sure they understand," said Judith.

Lew turned to Osborne. "All right, Doc. I hate to ask, but I sure hope you have the time to help me search this place. Every closet, every drawer, every shelf, every desk, and every computer—though I can have Dani check the computers. Thank goodness I have her to help out. It's times like this when I wish Loon Lake had a tax base that allowed for more manpower . . .

"I hate to pull Roger and Todd off their shifts. The minute I do that, we'll have six snowmobiles collide outside the Birchwood Bar—plus Todd has a wife and young children. He would never complain, but he's the last guy I want working overtime."

She gave Osborne a baleful look as she said, "And you know how much confidence I have in Roger." She rolled her eyes.

"Lew, I haven't had a chance to mention this, but Mallory surprised me this morning with the news that she's coming home. Not sure why or for how long, but it sounds like she'll be around for the next few days. So I am happy to help out, but I may need time to handle a few things back at the house. I'll know more this evening."

"Oh, well, Doc, if your daughter is coming home I better see if one of the sheriff's deputies—"

"Lew, stop," said Osborne, raising both hands as if to prevent her from calling the sheriff. "Of course I have time to help you search. We can get started right now if you wish. Yes, Mallory is coming, but I have no idea what she is up to and it wouldn't matter anyway. She is a big girl who can take care of herself."

He didn't add that spending time around Chief Lewellyn Ferris—whether on the department's ticket as a deputy, in the trout stream as her student, or in the boat as a fellow fisherman—

made his day. In fact, when she wasn't nearby, he wasted too much time thinking about her.

"If you're sure about that, Doc, I appreciate all the help you can give me. But before we start, let me give Dani a call. That slip of paper you found in Rudd's wallet—the one with the passwords on it—I'm sure she'll be all over that. If Rudd received any suspicious emails, she may be able to flag them. Let's hope anyway."

While Lew was on her cell phone giving Dani directions, Osborne decided to take a stroll through the spacious living room of the house. Looking up he saw the loft-like balcony where Judith was making her calls. It opened to a hallway lined with doors he assumed were bedrooms or closets.

From where he was standing on the ground floor, he glanced around and was struck by the integrity of the room's proportions: the ceiling height, the curve of the walls, even the dimensions of the windows. The design was the work of a talented architect, the kind who does not come cheap.

Early in Osborne's college years he had taken classes in studio art and discovered he loved working with wood and stone so much that he had entertained the thought of becoming a sculptor. That was until his father bluntly informed him: "Son, that is no way to make a living." He may not have followed his heart, but it didn't hurt that he brought to dentistry an eye for proportion: the ability to recognize when line, shape, and space are unified.

Continuing to explore the main room, he was aware of the furnishings, but nothing seemed overdone: The living space struck him as simple and lovely and utilitarian as a wooden dock over still water.

Just beyond the entrance to the room were two sofas, three groupings of armchairs, and a scattering of tables and lamps. To his left was a kitchen with white cabinetry masking shelves and appliances. The kitchen would have seemed sterile, but a wood plank floor and bright tea towels hanging from brass hooks added warmth.

Separating the kitchen from the comfortable living area was an all-white island set for dining with crisp china painted in bright yellows, light blues, and a cheery red. The table settings were so inviting he couldn't help but wonder what Rudd had planned to serve that evening. A sad smile crossed his lips as he turned away.

Color and warmth dominated the room as paintings, pottery, and gleaming brass sculptures were scattered across the walls and tables. While the furnishings had to be expensive they radiated a warmth and simplicity that made the interior feel cozy in spite of its size.

Lew walked up to stand behind him. "What a lovely home this is," she said, looking around. "If I was forced to move out of my farmhouse, I could live here." She brushed an appreciative hand across one of the sofas, which was plump and upholstered in a cream-and-spring-green pattern that reminded Osborne of summer grasses.

"Come on now," said Osborne, "you know you'll never leave your place." He dropped his voice to a whisper. "I keep asking and you keep refusing."

"I know," said Lew with a grin. "I'm just saying I like the feel of this place. I'm sure that the Tomlinsons must have loved it here. How very sad . . . " She didn't finish her comment.

"Well, you are out of luck, kiddo. Because if a house like this is what it would take to get you to move in with me—it is w-a-a-y out of my price range."

Lew squeezed his arm. "Thank heavens for that." She looked up at Osborne. "I'd say we're both happy where we're at."

"Really?" Osborne lifted an eyebrow as he gazed at the woman, the sight of whom in the early mornings when they shared a pot of coffee could make his heart feel like a bird. He watched as Lew crossed the room toward the far end, where the entire wall was of curved glass facing west across the frozen lake. There was not a seam in the wide, long wall of glass. Now *that* had to be very expensive.

"This place must have cost millions," said Osborne as Lew approached the window.

"Looks plenty cold out there," said Lew, shivering as she peered through the glass wall. Dark figures could be seen in the distance. "Those are some brave ice fishermen. Not sure a walleye is worth freezing to death."

"I'm with you, but tell that to our friend Ray," said Osborne. "Ray—who would rather ice fish on a day like today than from his boat on a warm July afternoon. Sometimes the world confounds me."

Lew had turned around and pointed up. Overhead wooden beams ended in a steeple of glass, echoing the diagonal timbered wings at the entrance. "I wonder if that's reclaimed wood?" she asked, referring to the beams and planks salvaged from old buildings and prized by the builders of expensive homes in the Northwoods. "I'll have to check with Judith. She might know. I've always wanted to see what reclaimed wood looks like."

Murmurs from the loft indicated Judith had reached someone by phone. While they waited for her to finish, Osborne and Lew walked in different directions along the perimeter of the large room. On the far end, opposite the glass wall, was a fireplace, its mantel sculpted from a slab of ebony granite. Gas logs burned brightly in its depths.

In a corner near the fireplace was a tall cherry cabinet containing a collection of fly rods—bamboo and fiberglass. "Lew, come here. Take a look at this," said Osborne with a wave toward the cabinet. Wood-handled fishing nets hung from brass nails on the walls, and two antique creels hung in each corner. Peering through the glass door, he and Lew studied the fly rods in silence.

After a moment, Osborne said, "Philip must have been quite the fly-fisherman."

"He certainly had taste in his gear," said Lew. "Here's the Winston rod designed by Joan Wulff—just like mine. I keep telling you, Doc, you should get one. That thumb indent could make a big difference in your casting. Winston may advertise it as designed for women, but I see plenty of men using it, too."

"Is that your kind way of criticizing my casting technique?" Osborne kidded her.

"That's Rudd's fly rod," said Judith, her voice catching Osborne off-guard. He hadn't heard her approach. "Coming down the stairs, I overheard you talking about the rods. I have the Joan Wulff rod, too, but mine is at home."

She walked over to join them in front of the cabinet. "Rudd and I took up fly-fishing together fifteen years ago—right after we met."

"*Fifteen years*," said Lew. "Wow, you two must have caught a few trout in your lifetime. Do you . . . " She paused to correct herself. "Sorry, I meant to say 'did' you fish around here? I'm surprised I haven't run into you on one of the local streams."

"Sure, we've fished the Elvoy, the Bois Brule, and the Middle Ontonagon—and every winter we liked going to Florida for bonefish, too. Our timing was always a bit strange because I had to take time off work—I'm a professor at the University of Wisconsin. Art history."

"So you and Rudd have known each other a long time," said Osborne, leaning back against one of the sofas near the cabinet.

"Yes, Rudd lost her husband and their little girl in a car accident right about the time my husband died of leukemia. We were in our early thirties and both working on PhDs in art history at the University of Minnesota when friends told us about one another, so we decided to get together for coffee and just hit it off.

"You know how it is," Judith went on, glancing over at Lew. "Some women—you know in an instant if you're on the same wavelength. Back then both of us agreed we had to find some way to deal with our grief and we wanted it to be healthy. Not booze, not men, not too much television, not losing ourselves in work—so we decided to learn how to fly-fish." Judith smiled at the memory.

"Neither of us had much money, but we had time off that summer so we booked ourselves into a weekend at the Wulff School of Fly Fishing out in the Catskills . . . It was a good antidote to grief for both of us.

"Every year since, even though she was teaching at the Art Institute in Chicago and I was in Madison, we've carved out time . . . " She sank into a leather armchair, dropped her face into her hands, and sobbed. Lew went to the kitchen for one of the colorful dishtowels, which she brought back and handed to her.

"I'm sorry," said Judith, her voice muffled in the towel. "I am so sorry . . . "

"Don't be," said Lew. "Doc and I have both lost people close to us. You have to cry sometime. Now is good. And this won't be the last time."

Osborne waited until Judith's tears had begun to subside. "Funny," he said as she wiped her nose and eyes. "You might appreciate knowing that I did the same thing, sort of."

"Really?" Eager to pull herself together, Judith encouraged Osborne to keep talking.

"My late wife got pretty upset when I happened to mention I was interested in learning to fly-fish—this was years ago. Her point being that I had already spent enough money on spinning rods and fishing tackle—not to mention too much time on the water fishing muskies. And she was right. So in the interest of staying married I didn't think about fly-fishing again until after she died."

"Oh, I'm sorry to hear you lost your wife. Was that recent?"

"Several years ago," said Osborne with a wave of his hand. He chose not to mention that Mary Lee's unexpected death from a bout of pneumonia that turned deadly in the midst of a blizzard had turned into a gift. There were times he felt bad about feeling that way—and times he didn't. "I'm doing fine today, but I struggled with the grief."

He didn't add that his grief was less a feeling of loss than one of being totally unmoored. Over their thirty years of marriage, he had grown so used to being bullied into following Mary Lee's directives (his only escape being the fishing boat) that without her demanding he "do this, do that," he sank into an aimless depression fueled with whiskey.

It was only his daughters' confronting him with the reality that he was going to kill himself—"or someone else on the road, Dad. Someone who doesn't want to die"—that made him get help. That courageous intervention by his two daughters had saved his life. He hadn't known he was so loved until then. Every morning since he had said a silent prayer of thanks.

"To be perfectly frank, Judith," said Osborne, "I ended up in rehab at Hazelden. When I got out, I felt like you and your friend must have: What can I do to fill my life in a positive way? After all, I have two daughters and grandchildren I would like to enjoy.

"It was right about then that I was cleaning my garage and found the fly rod I had hidden years earlier. On the advice of Ralph, who owns the sporting-goods store, I decided to give fly-fishing a try—and discovered how much I enjoy it. I'm not the best caster, but—"

"But you do catch fish," said Lew, interrupting. "Doc left out the important part of his story. He signed up for fly-fishing lessons and got me as his instructor."

"Yeah," said Doc, "Ralph set me up to meet 'Lou' down at the Prairie River late one afternoon. He said 'Lou' would get me started. And 'Lou' turned out to be . . . " He held out his right hand toward Lew.

"Me," said Lew. "My full name is Lewellyn, but friends call me 'Lew' and I have fly-fished for years. And not unlike you two, I took it up to deal with grief after I lost my son. He was the victim of a bar fight in his late teens.

"I'll never forget the day of my son's funeral. My grandfather handed me his fly rod and told me to stay in the water until I could feel my heart start to heal. Took two weeks, but Granddad was right. Since then I've become pretty good—won some awards for distance casting.

"At the time that I met Doc," Lew went on, "I had not yet been promoted to chief so I had time to moonlight as an instructor. No longer. Way too busy these days."

"So you both fly-fish," said Judith.

"Yep. In the winter I tie flies," said Lew. "Now, Judith, I hate to put an end to this conversation, but I have an investigation—"

"Of course you do. But tell me, please, what should I do? I was planning to stay here at the house, but I know I shouldn't do that until you've searched it."

"Correct," said Lew. "The Loon Lake Inn is right in the center of town. I suggest you get a room there, and you can walk over to one of the local restaurants for some dinner later."

Standing up, Judith said, "Food is the last thing on my mind. If you don't need me here any longer, I wrote down a list of Philip's children with their names and cell phone numbers. You've met Sloane. She is staying down the road at her place.

"Kenzie is the youngest and she lives with her husband, Greg. They have a house further down the road from Sloane.

"And then there is Tim," added Judith with a sigh of exasperation. "I am not sure where he is. I left him a voicemail asking him to call me. He likes to say he lives in Quebec, but he is here a lot.

Oh, and he also spends his winters on the island of Bonaire, so he may be there. I have no clue."

Looking down at the sheet of paper that Judith handed her, Lew said, "Thank you. This is very helpful. Does Rudd have siblings? Parents? Other people who need to be informed? I am happy to make those calls."

"No, just Philip's adult children, her stepfamily. Her folks are dead and no siblings. Except for me. Like I said, I was her closest friend."

"And heir. Isn't that what you told Sloane?" asked Lew.

"Afraid I exaggerated a bit," said Judith. "Her will puts me in charge of her assets but in the sense that her wishes will be carried out. I can tell you about that later . . . happy to. It's sure to infuriate some folks."

"So perhaps you should be careful?" Lew made it sound like she was kidding.

Judith paused and looked hard at Lew and Osborne. "If anything happens to me, nothing changes. The sooner Sloane, Tim, and Kenzie learn that—the better."

Judith picked up her coat and headed toward the door leading into the foyer.

"Judith, hold on just a minute," said Lew. "I want to run something by Dr. Osborne before you leave."

Lew motioned for Osborne to follow her into the kitchen, where she lowered her voice to say, "What would you think of the three of us getting dinner at the pub, Doc? If you have time, it could really speed up getting more background information on the Tomlinsons. I know nothing about that family, and you did say that you might have some information in your files. Maybe you could check on that before we meet for dinner?"

"Good idea," said Osborne. "Although . . . are you planning to tape our conversation? It can get pretty loud in the restaurant."

"Not yet," said Lew. "I want to keep this casual. But we can both take notes."

"You mean I can take notes," said Osborne, correcting her with a smile.

"If you wouldn't mind—you're awfully good at it."

"Sure."

Lew walked back across the room to where Judith stood waiting. "Dr. Osborne and I are planning to have dinner this evening at the Loon Lake Pub, which is not far from the Inn. Would you like to join us? That is, if you're not too tired. This has been a grueling day."

"I would. I would like that very much," said Judith. "I'm anxious for you to know more about Rudd before you meet Philip's family." She paused. "I'm not sure they'll be fair in their remarks about her."

"This won't be exactly social," said Lew. "One or both of us will be taking notes as we talk. Are you comfortable with that? If you aren't, I'll arrange for a more formal interrogation tomorrow."

"No, no, however you want to discuss things is fine with me," said Judith. "Frankly, I would just as soon not be alone right now. I feel so . . . flat. Company will be good."

Lew gave her a pat on the shoulder. "I know what you mean. Now, if you are okay driving yourself into town, get yourself a room at the Inn and I'll pick you up at six-thirty for dinner. But you'll have to look for a beat-up red Mazda pickup with a white topper—after office hours I drive my fishing truck."

"Sounds wonderful," said Judith with a grateful smile.

Chapter Eight

As he drove home to change for dinner after Lew had dropped him off back at the police station, Osborne thought back over the day. Seeing Sloane had jogged his memory of her mother, Caroline. He remembered that summer day long ago, when Caroline had rushed a teenaged Sloane into his office after she had fallen walking down to their dock and loosened one of her front teeth.

"You have to be very careful now, Dr. Osborne," Caroline had said, making her opinion of small-town dentists clear. "My Sloanie is the prettiest eighth grader in Shorewood Country Day, which is the most prestigious private school down where we live." Caroline spoke in a high-pitched, nasal tone, emphasizing the name of the private school and stroking her daughter's hair as she spoke, the implication being that no one else had a girl child quite so lovely, and certainly no children in Loon Lake could even hope to attend a private school.

The smirk on the teenager's face, paired with an overdose of eye shadow and lipstick, made it obvious she was her mother's daughter. Osborne doubted athletic activity of any kind would be high on this girl's list.

At first Caroline had refused to leave the room during Osborne's exam. "Mrs. Tomlinson," he had said while turning on his stool to face Caroline, "you have a choice. Either you leave this room while I examine your daughter or the two of you can leave and find another dentist. I do not allow parents in my room when

I have a patient in the chair. It is too distracting. Have I made myself clear?"

He had kept his voice low and authoritative as he told his lie: He didn't allow parents in the room for a reason that had nothing to do with distraction—too many adults had an unreasonable fear of the dentist and could be very effective at communicating that to their offspring. Take the parent out of the equation and most kids, whether aged five or fifteen, would listen to Osborne and relax. The few who had been so indoctrinated by fearful parents that they continued to quiver and cry would hear Osborne repeat the option of going to another dentist. That usually shut them up.

Caroline had acquiesced only after demanding that she be allowed to sit within hearing distance "in case Sloanie needs me." A small-boned woman with cramped features, hair too blonde, and a powdered face, Caroline had hit Osborne wrong the minute she had barged into his office that day. Nor did it help that she had been rude to his receptionist. But after a pause, while debating Osborne's directive, she had agreed to take a chair in the waiting room.

Osborne was relieved when he saw that Sloane's loosened tooth—so long as she didn't chew caramels or crunch down on peanut brittle—would heal itself. Meanwhile, it was August and chances were excellent that if she did have a problem it wouldn't happen until the family was back home in Lake Forest.

"Be careful, young lady," he had cautioned her. "You don't want me to have to pull that tooth and leave you with a gaping hole when you smile. Right?" Sloane's eyes had widened at the thought of an extraction: She would be very careful.

After parking his car in the driveway, Osborne let Mike, the black lab, out for a brief run in the snow. It was so cold that the poor dog hopped along on his paws until he had taken care of business.

His owner then trudged along the narrow path he had managed to shovel to the side entrance of his heated garage. Turning on the lights, he opened the door to the small room tucked behind the porch where he cleaned fish, the room where he kept the two tall oak file cabinets he had inherited when he took over his father's practice.

Once again, he was pleased that he had saved all the patient files from his thirty years of practicing dentistry in Loon Lake. The young dentist who had purchased his practice had scanned in the files of current patients before handing those records over to Osborne as well. The files were filled with the memories of people whose lives he had observed over years—some well lived, some disastrous. Little did a patient realize the secrets on display in their mouth: Dental hygiene is a map to one's habits elsewhere in life.

Oh yes—I'm sure at least one Tomlinson is in here, thought Osborne as his fingers moved quickly through the Ts in the file drawer marked "Summer Patients." The files were grouped into three clusters, each containing a decade's worth of summer emergencies.

Opening Sloane's file, he was surprised by how vivid was his memory of Caroline and a remark she had made that afternoon so long ago: "Yes, Paul," she had said with an air of deigning to speak to him on a personal level, "our place is quite lovely, but I am sorry to say that it's on Thunder Lake. All we have on our lake are muskie fishermen—I have to spend my whole summer around people I do not need to know."

That was when she had sighed and said, "If only Philip's grandfather had bought property over in Minocqua. You know, Elizabeth Taylor's brother, the art dealer, had a mansion there. Much classier summer crowd in that area . . . if you know what I mean."

And that reminded him of Mary Lee.

Over the years of their marriage, his wife had grown more rigid in her attitude toward their fellow residents in Loon Lake, expecting Osborne to spend his free time with the couples in her social clique, activities centered around dinner parties, golf, and bridge. When he would dare to excuse himself to spend time on the water, she was not happy.

His fishing buddies appalled her: "Paul, those men haven't seen a shirt and tie in years—much less a decent shave." To her mounting chagrin, Osborne chose his friends over hers, forgoing a shirt and tie to slouch into his well-worn khaki fishing clothes (which she made him hang on the back porch) and do his darnedest to avoid the razor.

After all, his philosophy of life (had she bothered to ask during the year of their courtship) was uncomplicated: He chose to practice dentistry so he could afford to fish. But she had never asked and he had never volunteered the information, so it was both their faults that over time their life together did not improve.

After glancing through the file on Sloane, Osborne checked through "Summer Patients" one more time, but she was the only Tomlinson in the drawer. So even though he had heard about the Tomlinsons, that must have been the only time he had met anyone in the family. He checked his watch: Oops—time to change and head back into town.

When Osborne arrived at the Loon Lake Pub and Café, Lew and Judith were already seated at a table near the back of the dining room. Lew would have chosen to sit there for privacy: It was hazardous to discuss anything personal in public in Loon Lake without checking over your shoulder to be sure you wouldn't be overheard by the wrong person.

Tonight the restaurant was half-empty, as few folks were inclined to leave the warmth of their homes given that the temperature was predicted to hit thirty below zero and the sidewalks were treacherous. But for the few who did brave the cold, the dining room was warmly lit and cozy with a zoo of deer mounts, foxes, pheasants, otters, and even a mink grinning down at them.

The two women, deep in conversation, greeted Osborne with smiles as he approached. He was pulling out the chair beside Lew when he saw a look of alarm cross Judith's face. Glancing back over his shoulder, he saw the problem. Shuffling between nearby tables and knocking chairs aside as it aimed directly for them was a humongous alien hiding in a snowmobile suit.

The creature was at least six feet tall, though a stuffed trout—head and tail extending out over the ears—added another six inches. The figure neared their table, boots clomping across the wood floor, until it reached the chair next to Judith's, where it plunked itself down.

As Judith reared back, Osborne raised a hand. "It's okay—it's just my neighbor. Contrary to appearances, he is not dangerous."

"Yo, Doc and Chief, " said the alien as he slapped deerskin mitts on the table, reached up to remove the fish from the top of his head, and turned to Judith saying, "Aren't you as lovely as a forget-me-not in spring." Judith's eyes widened.

"Judith Fordham," said Lew, "meet Ray Pradt—one of the deputies I've asked to help out with the investigation. You may have seen him photographing the site in front of the Grizzly Bear Café this morning.

"Ray, you should know it was Judith's very close friend, Rudd Tomlinson, who was killed by that logging truck." Lew spoke in a tone intended to alert Ray to the fact that this was not the time to be cute.

"That's quite the hat," said Judith, slightly more relaxed now that it had been confirmed that the interloper was familiar to her hosts.

"Thank you," said Ray. "This hat . . . " he paused as he always did in the presence of a female he hoped to impress, "is my motif . . . so to speak." Lew rolled her eyes at Osborne. They both knew what was coming next and were helpless to put a lid on it.

Ray had a habit of speaking in sentences sprinkled with pregnant pauses that Osborne swore were designed to hold listeners hostage. Apparently, not even the knowledge that someone in his audience might be grieving could get him to hurry words along.

"*Motif*? Not sure if that's the word you want to use," said Judith. "But then, I'm a college professor and way too critical when I hear someone abuse the English language. Maybe what you want to say is that the hat is your trademark, your *signature accessory*, maybe—"

"Signature *accessory*? I like that," said Ray interrupting her. "Adds weight to the image . . . *accessory* does. You see . . . the minute people see me and my hat . . . " Ray raised his index finger to emphasize his point, " . . . they know exactly my field of expertise."

"And I am afraid to ask what that is," said Judith, taking a sip of her wine. "But I'm going to guess it has something to do with fishing."

"Ah . . . indeed it does. And in the event that you . . . are a connoisseur of hats, you might like to know . . . I have a summer trout hat and this . . . is my winter trout hat," said Ray, tipping the hat over so she could see the snaps attaching furred earflaps that were nearly hidden by the brim of the worn leather cap holding the fish.

"And this . . . " he said, laying a delicate finger on a shiny fishing lure hanging from the neck of the fish, "this . . . is a memento of a fifty-two-inch muskie I caught years ago."

"Fifty-two inches! I don't know much about muskie fishing, but I do know that would be one large fish." As Judith spoke, Osborne could see the sadness that had creased her face all afternoon lighten a bit.

"Yes, it is. But much as I had hoped that fish was a record—it wasn't. What happened was . . . " said Ray, raising an instructive index finger, "I was casting when a family of ducklings swam near my boat and whomp! One disappeared . . . Sure sign of a monster lunker down below."

"Poor little duck," said Judith, hooked. Osborne threw a glance at Lew, who gave a shrug of resignation and motioned for the two of them to keep quiet.

"Well . . . yes and no," said Ray. "But I knew what to do next . . . I reached into my tackle box for a lure that looked just like a duckling—one with treble hooks on it—and cast it in the direction of the lunker . . . Wham! That fish hit hard. Gotta tell ya . . . I was sure I had a record."

"My gosh, I'll bet," said Judith, her eyes wide with admiration.

"But when I weighed that big girl . . . " longer pause now, "she came in at . . . four pounds."

"What on earth?" asked Judith. "How could that be?"

"She was full of feathers."

A moment of silence then Judith shook her head with a rueful laugh. "Okay, what else can you sell me?"

With a smile of satisfaction at having bamboozled his new friend, Ray crossed his arms and, looking straight at Judith, wriggled his ears. She looked down at the stuffed trout sitting on the table, then back at Ray. He wriggled his ears again.

"Give me a break—how do you do that?" she asked, sounding as delighted as a five-year-old at Christmas.

Before he could answer, Lew, anxious to get down to business, interrupted saying, "Ray, you called to say that you have something for me?"

"Yes, I do," said Ray, slipping out of his snowmobile parka and reaching into the top pocket of the insulated overalls he wore under the heavy jacket. He pulled out a long white envelope.

"Photos already?" said Lew. "Great, thank you."

As she opened the envelope, she said to Judith, "He may tell ridiculous jokes, but I don't know what I would do if I didn't have Ray—and Doc—to help out when unpleasant things happen. Between a three-man police force and the Wausau boys, who run a dysfunctional crime lab, I would be stuck. I doubt I'd ever solve a crime."

"Now, Chief, I appreciate the compliment, but don't forget our man Bruce" said Ray. "There's one of the Wausau boys I think you're going to need ASAP."

"Really?" asked Lew, sounding preoccupied as she slid the series of black-and-white photos from the envelope and leaned over to study the first.

What Lew did not mention was that Ray, aside from being an excellent photographer and fishing guide, was also a skilled tracker whom she would deputize when a crime scene needed the eye of an eagle—deputize in spite of his active misdemeanor file. While Ray was faithful in joining Osborne at the weekly AA meetings behind the door with the coffee pot etched on the window, he refused to give up one remaining vice: He was unequalled in his ability to track down inexpensive sources of marijuana.

But Lew had learned early on that there was a good reason to ignore that misdemeanor file: Ray's history of bad behavior enhanced his standing among other bad actors in the region. Enough so to give him a pipeline into the activities of the questionable characters who lived down logging lanes with no fire numbers. Ray could harvest information from sources neither she nor Officers Adamczak nor Donovan could tap.

As Lew continued to sort through the photos, Ray placed a zip-top bag onto the empty salad plate to her right. The zip-top held three cigarette butts. Lew raised her eyes to Ray's. "Yes," he said, "you can forget the rest of those Wausau boys, but you do need Bruce."

He looked over at Judith. "He's the best forensic tech they have down there. Plus," he grinned, "he loves to ice fish. You give him a call this evening and I guarantee he'll turn on a dime and give you nine cents back—he'll be here by morning."

Chapter Nine

Osborne, realizing how hungry he was and seeing no sign that Ray was likely leave soon, said, "Would you join us for dinner?"

"I would be as happy as the flowers in the field," said Ray.

"After you explain the cigarette butts," said Lew.

"Sure, but first the photos." As he spoke, Ray tipped his head with a questioning look toward Judith.

"It's all right," said Lew. "Not only is Judith a close friend of the victim's, she was driving up from Madison for a meeting with Rudd when Doc reached her by phone with the bad news.

"Now, Judith," said Lew, her voice lifting in warning, "you have got to keep what you are about to hear in confidence, especially if you're talking to any Tomlinson family members. Agreed?"

"No question—you can count on me to do whatever I can to help out." The intensity in Judith's eyes convinced Osborne that she was as determined to find the person behind Rudd's death as they were.

Pushing his chair closer to the table, Ray leaned forward over the photos. The auburn curls released from under his hat glistened in the glow of the votive candle near his plate. He was wearing a cream-colored Irish fisherman's sweater, which highlighted his ruddy cheeks above the curly beard that matched his hair, though streaks of grey were sneaking in. His eyes were so lively as he explained the photos to Lew that even Osborne had to admit his neighbor looked handsome.

"Now, Chief," said Ray, eyes on Lew, "remember you told me that young kid, the dishwasher, was looking out a window toward the driveway when he saw an old man go by?"

"Right . . . "

"Well, after photographing the victim and the logging truck, I took a walk back along that side of the building. That area isn't a driveway but a snow-covered patio that the café uses for summer dining, which means it isn't used in the winter—*but it was this morning.*"

"You found something," said Lew, her arms folded as she listened.

"Yes, I did. I found these footprints, which could only have been made this morning because they broke through the surface of the snowfall that we got last night." Ray passed the photo around so everyone could see.

"I followed the footprints through the snow all the way back to a snow bank along the street behind the parking lot. And there they stopped. Disappeared. The snow on the street is so packed down by the plows that boots don't leave an impression unless you're an elephant."

"Oh," Lew slumped back in her chair. "Damn. For a minute there . . . "

"Hold on," said Ray, raising his index finger. "The footprints stopped in a snow bank right in front of a house where a guy was out shoveling his walk. I asked if he might have seen anyone parked there earlier and he said he had. A red Honda sedan was parked there from about seven-thirty to shortly after nine this morning.

"He said he kept an eye on it, since the car didn't belong to any of his neighbors and he couldn't imagine why a visitor wouldn't use the parking lot that's right across the street instead of blocking the way for snowplows. Anyway, he said that watching from his living room window he could see that the person sitting in the car was some old guy 'with a real craggy face'—those are his words—who sat there smoking a couple cigarettes before he got out of the car and was gone for a while.

"So I walked over to where the guy said the car had been parked and found these three cigarette butts that might have been tossed out the window." Ray pointed to the zip-top on the salad plate. "Could be nothing, of course."

"Or, smoked by the old guy who pushed Rudd Tomlinson," said Lew. "Did you touch these yourself, I hope not?"

"Chief, how well do you know me? Of course not—and I did not use my fish glove either. I keep that box of nitrile gloves you gave me in my glove compartment, so I went back and got those before I picked these up. I was very careful."

"Good work, Ray. Anything else show up in the photos?"

"Not that I can see. You had a few bystanders come and go up until the truck was moved and the ambulance left. I did my best to get shots of everyone, but they looked to me like the people we know who work along Main Street: Jean from the gift store, Stan and Gert, who run the dry cleaner's, the waitresses from the Grizzly, and the gals from the Chamber office. Oh, and our favorite blowhard, Vern Steidl, who said his firm is doing some renovations on Dan Kelly's law office. He hung around for a while pontificating as usual, then talked up the kid who was washing dishes. Guess he fished with the kid's dad. That's all."

"Excuse me, folks," said Judith, rising from her chair. "Which way is the ladies room?" After she walked away, Lew turned to Ray. "What were you thinking, telling jokes to that poor woman? You know she just lost her best friend."

"I know, Chief," Ray raised serious eyes to Lew. Guess I just wanted to take some of the pain out of her face—for a few minutes. I was watching her this morning . . . " He shook his head in sympathy. "Maybe I did the wrong thing?"

"It worked," said Osborne, chiming in from the sidelines. "She's perked up for the moment, anyway. Really, Lewellyn, you know it can't hurt to help her take her mind off that awful scene this morning."

"I guess you're right," said Lew.

"I'm wondering why you're letting her sit in on this discussion," said Ray. "I hate to say it, but you don't know that she didn't hire someone—I mean, the Tomlinsons are a very wealthy family. I'll bet there's a hell of a lot of money involved here."

Lew glanced over her shoulder to be sure Judith wasn't on her way back to the table. "Something I learned when I was studying criminal psych was that the person guilty of committing a premeditated murder will tend to be content, even relaxed, after the crime. And for good reason: they just got the person bugging them off their back.

"Do either of you have the sense that Judith Fordham is anything but devastated by her friend's death?" When neither Ray nor Osborne contradicted her, she said, "I'm not saying I'm a hundred percent right, but I'm willing to go with my intuition on this. Plus, she's not hesitant to share her opinions of the Tomlinson family members. I'm anxious to hear what she can tell us."

Judith returned to the table just as the waitress showed up to take their order. After ordering and requesting that all their dinners be put on one bill, Lew said, "My turn to be excused. I have Bruce Peters's home number in my phone and I'd like to see if I can't get him up here tomorrow. If not, I'll have Roger run these butts down to him. The sooner I can get a good DNA sample, the better. Back in a sec."

Lew was back within two minutes. "Had to leave Bruce a voicemail. Told him I could use his help tomorrow if at all possible. Oh, and I promised Bruce some ice fishing, so I'm pretty sure we'll hear from him. That work for you, Ray?"

"Yep," said Ray. "Why . . . don't we see . . . how the day . . . goes. Miss Judith, here, has probably never . . . ice fished . . . in her life. Have you?"

"No. I fly-fish," said Judith. "No ice fishing. Why?"

"Well, I'm thinking . . . you might like to join us . . . me and Mr. Peters."

"Oh." Judith looked taken aback but not unhappy at the thought. "But I don't have the right clothes. Don't I need warmer clothing like what you're wearing?"

Before anyone could answer her question, Judith said, "Wait, I almost forgot something that might get in the way of going fishing. While I was waiting for Chief Ferris to pick me up, I had a call from Philip's daughter, Kenzie, who said her brother, Tim, is visiting this week before he leaves for two months in Bonaire, and she wants to have a family meeting at her home in the morning to plan some sort of memorial for Rudd."

"The *family* wants to plan a memorial? How do *you* feel about that?" asked Osborne, remembering Sloane's hostile response to Judith and the news of Rudd's death.

Judith tipped her head sideways and pressed her fingers against her eyelids before taking a deep breath and saying, "This isn't kind of me, but those people . . . well, when I'm around them I feel like I'm in a roomful of spiders."

Lew stared at her. "Then don't do it—especially if you're not comfortable with those people."

"Believe me, when they learn that I am the executor of Rudd's will, there will be fireworks. It won't be pleasant and I'm not sure I'm ready for that yet."

"I have a suggestion," said Lew. "Let's figure out a way for Doc and me to be there with you. Not only do I have to search your friend's home before any family members can have access, but I need to speak with each one in private. I want to know where they were at the time that Rudd was hit and if they have any idea how and why this might have happened to their stepmother.

"The way I work, I like Doc to sit in on the interviews with me. He's my backup in case something goes wrong when I'm taping: He takes good notes." Lew grinned over at Osborne.

"I see," said Judith, her voice thoughtful. "What if I say that I've invited you to come in order to give the family all the details and see if they have questions for you, Chief Ferris? That opens it up for you to arrange the interviews and, maybe, deflect their attention from me. Frankly, I'll feel better having you as my backup." She gave a soft, sad smile.

"What about me?" asked Ray. "Spiders make great bait."

"That is not true," said Lew.

"So? I tried. Seriously, if you want me there, let me know."

"I do want you there," said Lew, "but outdoors. If you and Bruce can check any outer buildings as well as walk the Tomlinson property in case someone was stalking the victim, that would save me time. Doc will help me investigate Rudd's house, which we'll start first thing in the morning before taking a break to go with Judith to meet the family. Does that work for everyone?"

"Sorry to interrupt," said their waitress, who had walked up just as Lew asked her question. "Does anyone want coffee? Dessert?" All four hands went up.

Chapter Ten

"Umm, that was good," said Judith, finishing off a slice of apple pie. "Before I head back to the inn I wonder if you folks would like a little background on how Rudd and Philip met, especially since his children never warmed to her. That may help explain their attitude toward me, anyway."

"I am very interested," said Osborne, "since I think Philip was about twenty years older than Rudd, wasn't he?"

"Twenty-two to be exact," said Judith. "He was sixty-nine when he died."

"Why would that be important, Doc?" asked Lew. "I mean, you're eleven years older than me and I don't think your daughters are upset with that."

"It's not the age difference, Lew, so much as they strike me as such different people—"

"Yes and no," said Judith. "Philip and Rudd had something unusual in common. Both were cancer survivors and that's how they met—while getting chemo at the hospital over in Green Bay. That was five years ago. Their treatments were successful for a while and they had two terrific years together before Philip's cancer returned.

"On the other hand, they could not have had more different lives before they met. Rudd grew up in Eagle River. She was an only child who lost her parents early, so she rarely went back to visit her hometown. Even after her husband and their little girl were killed in the car accident, which is when we became friends, she stayed close to the university and her research.

"The irony of her life is that just when she got a major grant to write a book on the artist Georgia O'Keeffe and the Wisconsin influences on her art, Rudd was diagnosed with lymphoma. That was when she decided to come home. The woods and the water and the little cottage that she had inherited from her parents suddenly seemed the most comforting place to be. At that point, my friend's prognosis was not good, but she agreed to give chemotherapy a try. I have to hand it to her—Rudd was an optimist.

"Right about that same time, Philip was diagnosed with prostate cancer. He was told he needed aggressive chemotherapy if he was going to survive. He wasn't sure if he wanted to go through all that. He hadn't had an easy life."

"Come on, I find that hard to believe," said Ray. "My father used to take me fishing up on Thunder Lake. He told me the Tomlinsons owned almost the entire lake. The great grandfather was the 'barbed wire baron' of the North—there wasn't a roll of fencing that didn't come from one of the Tomlinson factories."

"You're right about that," said Judith. "And Philip was the heir to that fortune. Like Rudd, he was an only child, and during his youth, his father diversified into paper mills and railroads, so when he died, Philip inherited over a hundred million dollars. But he had been a lonely child who grew up going to boarding school and summer camp. He rarely saw his parents.

"Sure, most people think he should have been happy, that he never had to work, but for Philip that extreme wealth was a curse. He told Rudd he hated never having the satisfaction of accomplishing something—just like he hated his wife. And two of his three children."

"Whoa, let's stop right there," said Lew, glancing over her shoulder to make sure she wasn't being too loud. "He hated his wife? But they had children. You don't have children with some-one you hate."

Even as she spoke, Lew knew she was wrong. She remembered her own fury at the man who had fathered her two children: the cute, reckless teenager who had morphed into a shiftless drunk. A drunk she shed the minute she could earn a modest living as a secretary at the local paper mill before, eventually, putting herself through school so she could enter law enforcement. So, yes, you can have children with someone you hate—it's just that you may not experience that hatred until too late.

"Philip was married young—I think he was only twenty-five. He met Caroline at a friend's wedding. He thought she was very pretty, which she was. She thought he was very rich, which he was," said Judith with a wry laugh. "Surprise, surprise—guess who announced she was pregnant three months after they started dating.

"Philip told Rudd that Caroline's parents allegedly were scan-dalized and demanded that he marry her, but he always suspected her mother had encouraged her to trap him into the marriage. And back in the day that's what a responsible young man did. So they eloped. Seven months later, Sloane arrived.

"From what he told Rudd—and who knows what the real story is because we all know the definition of a dysfunctional fam-ily is 'more than one person'—Caroline went on to have two more children over the next ten years and then she locked her bedroom door. Not figuratively, either. Whatever her reasons, now that she had three children, plenty of money, and a lovely home in Lake Forest—she felt she no longer needed to put up with Philip.

"On the other hand, she refused to divorce him and he didn't push it. His father had kept a mistress for years, and since both Philip's parents were still alive, Philip didn't want the Tomlinson history of marital misery selling Chicago papers. Maybe he was too private for his own good.

"But with the estrangement from Caroline, he had no reason to stay in Lake Forest. He could manage the family fortune from anywhere, so he moved up north. At first he lived in the old lodge built by his grandfather, but when Caroline decided that she and the children should spend the summers there, too, Philip bought himself an old Airstream house trailer and put it down twenty feet from the lake and far away from the family."

"A house trailer? That seems odd. He could certainly afford to build another house, couldn't he?" asked Lew.

"Yes, but he loved being right on the water, and I think he took great satisfaction in the fact that his trailer appalled Caroline. She was *not* going to take visitors down to a trailer home, so he knew he was safe. And it was cozy. Philip was a good cook and he had outfitted the little kitchen just the way he wanted. His fishing boat and canoe were right there—"

"You'll have to see my place," Ray interrupted. "I know just how the guy felt. Sounds just like my trailer."

"Except yours has a monster fish painted on it," said Lew. "Yours is a house trailer designed to frighten small children."

"Really?" Judith sounded intrigued. "Hmm. Well, let me finish because I know it's getting late. Are we the last ones here?" She looked around.

"There are people in the bar," said Osborne. "They don't close until midnight."

"But you folks have had a long day," said Judith. "I'll talk fast. By the time Rudd met Philip, he had been living in the house trailer for years. He was a widower. Caroline had stumbled one day, fallen down the basement stairs in the old lodge, and died of a skull fracture. By that time, the children were grown. Sloane was on her second marriage, and Tim was alleged to be an artist living summers in Quebec and spending winters painting and scuba diving in Bonaire.

"Tim, for the record, was his mother's favorite. That woman saved every drawing, every painting he did since he was a toddler. When Rudd and Philip decided to have the lodge torn down for structural reasons, not to mention bad memories, it took an entire day to empty the two rooms where Caroline had stored every piece of art that her son had produced. But it was the kind of stuff that only a mother would love. Philip offered to have it boxed up and shipped to Tim's home in Quebec. When Tim didn't answer his dad's phone calls and emails—off it went to the dump.

"That may explain why Tim had the hardest time adjusting to Rudd. I mean, Rudd and I know fine art—as scholars and as professors schooled in the studio-art experience. We know when someone has a good eye, a command of craft, a genuine talent. Tim has never taken a formal class in any of the arts—not even drawing. His mother told him he was brilliant and he believed her.

"In my humble opinion," added Judith, looking around the table, "he does have one outstanding talent—he's 'Mister Answer Man.' He knows it all and doesn't hesitate to let you know how pathetic you are."

"You love the guy, right?" said Ray with a chuckle. "But I know exactly what you mean. This brings back a memory from when I was eight years old. My dad, who was a surgeon, knew Philip Tomlinson from when he set a broken finger for the guy.

"So this one day, Dad made me go fishing with him and the Tomlinsons, Philip and Tim. Tim was older and bigger than me and he kept pushing me around in the boat. We went swimming later and he thought it was hilarious to hold my head underwater until I just about drowned. Guy was a bully and a jerk."

"Still is," said Judith. "Rudd could barely stand to deal with him.

"Then there is Kenzie, the youngest and the nicest of the three, but I think that's because she's bipolar or, maybe, borderline schizophrenic. Who knows? She's always on some drug that keeps her pretty spacey. She is married to a really sweet guy from Loon Lake whom her mother hated. Kenzie was the only one of the three children to whom Philip was close."

"A lot of hate in the family," said Ray, pouring himself more coffee.

"I don't understand," said Lew. "Why did Philip not care for his children? That seems a bit extreme."

"I thought the same, but Rudd said that he told her that Caroline was so overprotective of the children that he was rarely allowed much time with them. If you think about how he grew up—as an only child whose parents assigned his care to maids, nannies, camp counselors, and boarding schools—I'm sure part of the problem was Philip's. He didn't know how to be close to his children.

"By the time they were teenagers, the marriage was a shambles and he considered the kids to be—and these are the words he used—'rude, entitled little brats, just like their mother.'"

"Philip didn't hold back, did he?" said Ray as he passed the thermal coffee pot around the table. "Doc, want a refill?"

"Nope, one more cup and I'll never get to sleep," said Osborne.

"I'll have a touch," said Lew. "I have paperwork to take care of before I can sleep. Thank you, Judith, this is quite the happy family you've just outlined for us."

"One last little item you should be aware of before you meet the crew. And, by the way, I know I'm prejudiced and I am well aware your impressions of the family may be—and maybe should be—very different from mine, but if I seem too critical, I loved Rudd—"

"We know that," said Lew. "You're saving us time in understanding the dynamics of the family."

"See . . . " Judith paused, "where I am really going is that I don't think that family meeting tomorrow has anything to do with planning a memorial for their stepmother—they just want to know where the money is. And they are in for an unpleasant surprise.

"This goes back to when Caroline was still alive. In the event that he died first, Philip didn't trust her not to leave everything to the kids, which he told Rudd was the last thing he wanted. So he sold all the family assets and established a generous income for Caroline, but only after she agreed to write a will of her own that restricted the children to receiving just half a million each.

"He placed the rest of his money in a separate trust and, on marrying Rudd, he named her as the sole beneficiary of his estate. It overruled any will that may have been left—by him or Caroline. Philip's entire estate then was included in that trust and it all went to Rudd.

"That infuriated his children. So Tim hired a lawyer last year to contest the trust beneficiary." Judith paused. "Rudd told me yesterday that Tim learned just two weeks ago that he had no hope of changing anything—it is a rock-solid legal document."

"But what happens now that Rudd is dead?" asked Lew.

"That's what I have to tell the family tomorrow. Rudd set up a trust to be administered by me, and my job is to see that the museum is built, the art purchased, and the endowment managed so the museum is always open to the public. That news," said Judith with a grimace, "will be hard for Philip's kids to hear, especially Tim. I have no doubt they think they are about to inherit a windfall."

"You have mentioned a museum a couple times now," said Osborne. "Is this something local? Or an institution in Minneapolis? What is it exactly?"

"It's an art museum to be built on the Tomlinson property, with paintings and drawings by two artists who Rudd and Philip both loved: Georgia O'Keeffe and Helen Frankenthaler. Paintings by both are very expensive, so Rudd anticipated having just one or two by each—but a significant collection of drawings and studies. I know this sounds a bit much."

"If this was about pictures by Gary Larson, like *The Far Side*, I'd know what you're talking about," said Ray. "Or even a museum for antique snowmobiles, but you just lost me." Osborne and Lew nodded in agreement.

"Trust me, there was a method to their madness in planning this," said Judith. "Once they got past their health issues, Rudd and Philip discovered they had a lot in common. They loved the outdoors and fly-fishing, but they also loved art, which they discovered by accident.

"One day when they were sitting near one another while getting chemo, they both reached for a copy of *ARTnews* magazine, which someone had left behind, and started to chat. That sparked their interest in each other. Over the next three months, they continued to chat during their treatments and it was always about art or movies or fly-fishing. They were a dear pair, really."

"Then, during the two years they had together during which they both had quite good health, they decided to invest Philip's money in a new museum to be built on Philip's property and focus on O'Keeffe and Frankenthaler. Rudd already owned a print by Frankenthaler, and Philip had a Georgia O'Keeffe painting that he had inherited. They were going to call it The Tomlinson Museum.

"Philip was really excited. He told me he felt for the first time in his life that he could do something important. Rudd, of course, loved the idea. She said that growing up in Eagle River the only art she ever saw was what she called 'cottage porn'—paintings of ducks, deer, or cottages bathed in moonlight.

"She wanted kids growing up in the Northwoods to have a chance to see that all art doesn't have to be realistic—it can be weird, it can be dots and straight lines, it can be abstract splashes of color, it can be shapes that look like something out of a strange dream. She wanted people, especially kids, to learn to see beyond the obvious."

"Will the museum be in the house?" asked Osborne, thinking of the swooping wings at the entrance.

"No. The house will become the administrative offices, and the museum will be built in the big field you see driving in. The building Rudd bought in town was for temporary offices. The architect who designed the house has already drawn up plans for the museum.

"And that's what I am now in charge of. Rudd wanted the museum built, and together we've been talking to curators and art dealers. As of the stock market today, there is enough money for a twenty-million-dollar building and four or five works by each artist. Rudd's trust leaves around one hundred fifty million dollars. "

"This will be unpleasant news for Sloane, Tim, and Kenzie. Correct?" asked Lew.

"Afraid so."

"Very interesting," said Ray, getting to his feet. "Please excuse me, folks. I have to get home for my dogs."

"Sorry to have bent your ear for so long," said Judith, "but I thought it would help to understand the family dynamic that may occur tomorrow morning."

"We will plan to see you in the morning around ten," said Osborne, pushing in his chair.

"Yes," said Lew, "and I will have a good excuse for why we are showing up."

Judith watched Ray leave before turning to Lew and Osborne. "So he really lives in a trailer shaped like a fish?"

"Heavens, no," said Lew, laughing. "The trailer is painted dark green with long teeth—it's painted to *look* like a muskie. Summers, Ray is a fishing guide, and his clients get a kick out of driving up to a big fish."

"He lives right next door to me," said Osborne. "Looking out the window at Ray's place used to drive my late wife nuts."

"He's like a walking piece of folk art," said Judith. "You wouldn't happen to know how old he is—and is he involved with anyone?"

"He's thirty-two," said Osborne, "same age as Mallory, my oldest daughter. As far as involved with anyone? I don't know. Do you, Lew?" Lew shrugged.

"I'll bet he is," said Judith. "That is one handsome guy even if he does wear a fish on his head. Fun." With that she walked off to get her coat, which was hanging on the coat rack at the entrance to the restaurant.

"Don't tell me she's interested in Ray," said Osborne with a sigh. "How does he do it? Plus, she has to be at least ten to fifteen years older—" Lew punched him in the arm.

Twenty minutes later, Osborne pulled into his driveway and before hitting the button for his garage door, he noticed the lights were on in his kitchen. Sure enough, right next to his parking spot in the garage was Mallory's car. He hadn't realized that she would be driving up so soon.

"Hi, Dad," said his daughter, jumping up from the kitchen table where she was eating a peanut-butter sandwich. "Did you get my voicemails?"

"Oh, darn. I'm afraid I forgot to check my phone during dinner."

"That's okay. I have great news. I just took this new job as the director of marketing for an art museum being built up here by a woman I met during a seminar I took at the Art Institute. She married some wealthy guy who died and left her a fortune—"

"Rudd Tomlinson."

"Yes. How did you know?"

Osborne pulled out the chair beside his daughter and sat down.

Lew unlocked the front door to her farmhouse and pushed it shut against the wind howling outside. It had been an hour since she'd dropped off Judith, completed the office paperwork, and finally heard back from Bruce Peters with the Wausau Crime Lab.

"Hey, Chief Ferris, got your message," Bruce had said. "How are those walleyes biting? You getting any ice fishing in?"

"Not if I can help it," said Lew. "I do not ice fish. But I do have a problem you can help me with and, if you can, I know someone who will be happy to help you freeze your fingers jigging."

"Not my buddy Ray."

"Yes, your buddy Ray." And with that, she filled Bruce in on the events of the day and the discovery of the cigarette butts. "Maybe nothing, but then again . . . "

"You know that DNA testing will take time, Chief. Like a couple weeks or longer, but I'll head your way in the morning. I'll make a few calls, too. We might be able to speed it up—we'll see."

"I appreciate that, Bruce. See you tomorrow."

Chapter Eleven

As she turned up the thermostat on the new furnace, Lew realized how tired she was. It had been a long day. Just as she wrapped herself in the warm bathrobe that Osborne had given her for her birthday, she heard a knocking on the kitchen door.

Lew was startled. Who on earth at this hour? She checked her watch. It was after ten. Not the time a rational person, not even someone selling Avon products, chooses to drop in for a visit. Plus, everyone who knew her was well aware that she insisted people, even close friends like Doc, call before coming by. Judges and police officers had learned the hard way that unsolicited visits could be dangerous.

Tiptoeing into the bedroom, Lew reached into the holster for her Sig Sauer pistol. Edging her way back through the living room toward the kitchen, she stayed away from the windows. She paused beside the kitchen door, gun ready. Whoever it was knocked again.

"Who is it?"

"Hello, Mrs. Ferris, you don't know me. Charlene Murphy. I know it's late, but I'm on my way home from work and I was hoping to ask you a couple questions about your late husband?"

"I don't have a *late* husband." Lew held her breath.

"Your former husband, I mean—Mr. Robert Ferris?" Letting her intuition kick in, Lew relaxed ever so slightly. The woman sounded sincere, if misinformed.

"We've been divorced for years. I don't know anything about the man, though I did hear he died a while back, but that was long after we broke up. And that that's all I know. So please leave."

"He's my birth father. I'm adopted and trying to find my birth mother. I think, I'm pretty sure, you can help me." Ohmygod, thought Lew, what next?

She opened the door to the porch a crack. "All right," said Lew, aware she sounded testy. "I doubt I can help you. And if I could, why would you come out here so late?" The lights from the kitchen illuminated the face of the young woman on the porch. She had worried blue eyes and cheeks bright red from the cold.

"You're right. It is too late. Maybe I could come back another time? I live in Tomahawk, but I manage an office in Loon Lake that just opened, so I drive this way every night on my way home. I work late most nights. This is the first time I've seen lights on, so I thought I'd see if you were home. I guess you travel a lot?"

"You can see my lights from the highway?" Lew knew that wasn't true.

"Um, I know your fire number, so I've been pulling into your driveway until I could see your house and whether someone was home. Guess maybe I was trespassing? I am so sorry if I was, but I didn't know any other way to reach you. You aren't in the phone book."

"No, I am not. You're right about that."

Convinced the woman was no threat, Lew hid her gun in a drawer under the kitchen counter and opened the door.

"Come on, step inside before we both freeze." The young woman stepped in, her eyes grateful. "Here," said Lew, pulling out two chairs from her small kitchen table, "sit down. Tell me: What makes you think that my ex-husband, whom I divorced many years ago, might be your birth father?"

"I grew up with a family who said they adopted me after a priest told them of a man looking for a home for a newborn.

The man signed all the papers but didn't name the mother of the child. He's dead, but I was able to get his name from the people at the church rectory: Robert Ferris. Wasn't he your husband? I thought maybe you would know the woman or women that he knew after your divorce. If you do, then I hope to find the one who is my mom. I'm sure it sounds goofy, but I just want to know exactly who I am. You know, health information for myself and my children, maybe what my mother looked like." She was about to break into tears.

Lew reached over to pat the woman's hand as she said, "I'm sorry to disappoint you, but once you divorce someone you do your best to avoid them. Stay out of the line of fire, if you know what I mean.

"After we split, Rob moved away and whatever he did was none of my business. My daughter did see him occasionally and said he had many women friends. She's the one who told me he had died. That's as much as I know and I'm sorry."

"Oh, I see. Well, sorry to have bothered you like this. You were kinda my last hope." She stood up, defeat in her eyes.

"Charlene, there are private detectives who might be able to help you."

"They are so expensive. But you're right. Pretty soon I'll have paid off my school loans and I'll be able to afford one."

"Sounds like you have a good job . . . "

"I do." The young woman's voice brightened as she stood up to leave. "And I love the people here. You know, we have three new mines in the area and we're one of the top suppliers of sand to the companies fracking for oil in North Dakota."

"Speaking of detectives, how did you find me? How did you know my fire number?"

"Oh, that was easy. I manage the new regional office for the Wisconsin Silica Sands Mining Company in town. We have all the land records, and I was looking in the plat book at properties around here when I saw your name. I knew that my birth father was from here, so when I saw Lewellyn Ferris I figured you might have been married to Robert Ferris—or be a relative, anyway."

"I'm listed in the plat book?" Lew was stunned. She thought all her personal information was confidential—no phone listings, no cable-television records, no trash pick-up—even her mail was delivered to a P.O. box. When she took the position with the Loon Lake Police it was understood that those personal details would be kept in confidence for one simple reason: People arrested, convicted, and sent to prison too often seek retribution later. Police Chief Lewellyn Ferris was one of many people in the law enforcement and judicial systems who preferred anonymity. And now she was in the plat book, which was available to any razzbonya with a license to hunt. Hunting meant carrying a gun. This was not good.

"Yes, you're in the plat book," she heard Charlene saying, "because this property is over five acres in size. That's why."

"Well, I'm going to talk to the county and get that changed," said Lew. "Can you see that I'm removed from the records used by your company?"

"Sure. Everything is digital, so it should be easy to delete your name from the database, but why?"

"Because I am chief of the Loon Lake Police and I do not want every convicted felon getting out of prison to have my home address. I guess you didn't know who I was when you drove out here."

"Gosh, no. I must have scared you."

"Let's just say you put me on alert."

Lew was about to open the door for the woman to leave when she paused. "I have a thought, Charlene. Let's do a quid pro quo. You take my name off the plat-book database and I'll arrange for you to meet with Dani Wright, an intern of ours who is a whiz at Internet searches. I'll see if she has the time to do some freelance work, and maybe she can help you for a lot less than a private detective would charge. Since I have Robert Ferris's Social Security number, you two will have somewhere to start. Want to try that?"

"Are you serious? Sure. I'll try anything. And I will get your name off the plat-book database tomorrow morning. Don't you worry, Chief Ferris."

"I appreciate that, Charlene. I will talk with Dani in the morning and tell her to expect a call from you. Here's the number where you can reach her when you're ready."

Meanwhile in Osborne's kitchen, Mallory, a pained expression in her eyes, listened as her father told her what had happened that day. As he finished describing the situation surrounding Rudd Tomlinson's death, he asked, "Have you met the woman who was her right hand—Judith Fordham?"

"Yes, sort of. I was on a conference call with Rudd—she insisted I call her by her first name—and Judith Fordham. That's when I was hired. So I haven't met Judith in person, but—"

"You will tomorrow. Given what I heard tonight from Judith, she is going to need help. Lots of help. She is planning to build that museum in spite of Rudd Tomlinson's death."

"So I may have a job after all?" Mallory's face eased with relief.

"Judith said that Rudd put everything in a trust for the museum and named Judith as the chief administrator. Unless the two of you don't get along, I think you will have a very interesting job."

He didn't add that handling the Tomlinson family might be part of it. Nor did he add that he liked the idea of having ears he could trust, ears Lew could trust, close to what would be happening with the millions of dollars earmarked for the museum.

Mallory sat thinking. "Dad," she said finally, "do you think Rudd was killed for the money?"

"I can't imagine otherwise. And likely by someone not smart enough to know that getting their hands on the Tomlinson fortune might not be as easy as it may have looked."

"In that case, wouldn't whoever was behind Rudd's death be after Judith next?"

"Could be. We'll know more tomorrow when Judith meets with the family. She said they said they've called the meeting to plan a memorial service for their stepmother, but she's convinced it is really to find out if the money now goes to each of Philip Tomlinson's adult children.

"Chief Ferris and I will 'drop in,' so to speak, as a preliminary to examining Rudd and Philip's home, which has been secured as a crime scene. I think I'll ask Lew to check with Judith beforehand—she may want you to be there, too. You are working for her, right?"

"Technically, I was starting next Monday, but that's a good idea. By the way, Dad, don't let my staying here get in the way of your entertaining. I'll come and go from downstairs until I can get my own place—"

"*Entertaining?*"

"You know—you and Chief, I mean you and Lew, I mean . . . "

Osborne sighed. "I'm too old-fashioned, I guess. It is a little embarrassing to have Lew over when you're here. It's that propriety I picked up from the Jesuits years ago. And Lew may be a little uncomfortable, too."

"Look, Dad. I know you two enjoy being together, having breakfast together. I will stay out of the way, I promise. Maybe I'll tromp through the snow and have coffee with Ray."

She grinned, knowing full well that Osborne always worried that she might hook up permanently with his crazy neighbor, with whom she had had a fling not too long ago.

"You might want to knock first," said her father.

"Really."

"You know Ray better than I do. Mallory, I am pooped. I'm going to let the dog out and get some sleep. Good night."

"Night, Dad. Thanks for not being upset that I showed up so kind of unannounced."

"I think it is good that you will be here. See you in the morning, kiddo."

After letting Mike out for the last time, Osborne stood at the back door while the dog leapt along the shoveled walkway to the garage. The icy path was so cold that the lab hopped like a rabbit. Osborne gazed at the winter moon overhead, listening as the snow fell in whispers.

Chapter Twelve

When Lew, Osborne, and Mallory walked into the Loon Lake Inn at nine the next morning, Judith was surprised to see Mallory. "I never connected the name Osborne between you and your dad," she said.

"And I was—I am still—stunned to hear what happened to Mrs. Tomlinson," said Mallory. "Believe me, I understand if you have to tell me there is no position for me. I can't imagine—"

"Oh, but there is," said Judith. "This is part of what I have to tell the family today. Rudd signed documents months ago saying that after her death she wanted her estate to be used to run the Tomlinson Museum. I'm to be in charge and I will be in desperate need of your help, Mallory. I would love for you to come with me this morning when I meet with the family. It'll give you a heads-up on some issues we may be facing. Do you mind?"

Both women looked relieved. Mallory turned to Osborne. "So, Dad, be patient. I'll start looking for an apartment or a condo tomorrow. Maybe I can find a cabin to rent."

"Oh, don't do that yet," said Judith. "Once Chief Ferris has completed her investigation of Rudd's home, I think you and I can move into the guest quarters—at least until we have the legal issues settled. Plus, Rudd purchased a number of important artworks from private dealers, and I can use your help with the organizing and cataloging."

"Great," said Mallory. "I think we should plan to get a press release out to the arts community explaining that Rudd Tomlinson's death won't put an end to her plans for the museum, too."

"Good point." A smile crossed Judith's face. "See, we're moving forward already."

As she sat listening to the two women, Lew thought back to her conversation with Dani early that morning. She had alerted her to a possible call from a Charlene Murphy asking for help locating her birth mother—and to the fact that Lew had suggested Dani might be able to help on a freelance basis. In a brusque tone, she had added that Charlene's birth father was Lew's former husband—and hoped Dani wouldn't ask any questions. Dani gave her a long look before she apparently decided not to say a word. Lew was appreciative. Some details about her private life did not have to be shared with staff.

By nine-thirty they had finished breakfast and were on their way to the Tomlinson family meeting. Osborne and Lew followed Judith's car past Rudd's home to a two-story frame house about a third of a mile down the road. The house was grey-shingled, with white trim and a red door. It looked brand-new.

They parked behind Judith along the road, as the driveway already held three cars and a large Ford pickup. A stiff wind blasted their faces as they stood waiting for Judith and Mallory to climb out of the other car and join them.

"Where are we?" asked Lew, pulling the collar of her parka up close to her face.

"This is Kenzie and Greg Steidl's home," said Judith. "After their mother died, each of the siblings inherited a waterfront lot. That plus half a million dollars, which certainly helped Kenzie build this place."

"Kenzie, by the way, was the only one at home when her mother fell, fractured her skull, and died on the basement steps. It was Kenzie who had to watch the EMTs try to revive Caroline.

"After going through all that, Philip told Rudd that he tried to get Kenzie to get professional help. He felt the trauma of her mother's death was causing her to behave strangely. After Philip's death, Rudd made sure Kenzie saw a good psychiatrist over in the cities. She still sees someone, maybe a psychotherapist."

"I know Greg and his father, Vern," said Osborne, "and I knew Greg was married, but I didn't know his wife was a Tomlinson. Interesting."

He didn't add that Vern Steidl was the type of man he detested. Ray might call him a blowhard, but Osborne found him to be a buffoon. He was so smart that he once registered to run for a position on the Loon Lake Planning and Zoning Commission— before the town clerk in charge of printing ballots pointed out the obvious potential for a conflict of interest when a guy running a construction company is in a position to vote on property issues affecting his competition. Even more irritating, Vern had a habit of showing up at McDonald's for morning coffee and holding forth with bombastic rhetoric on local politics as if he had a clue what he was talking about. But the worst was Vern's pride in hunting bears with dogs trained to chase and tree the animals, a sport that turned Osborne's stomach.

More than once, Osborne himself had been out hunting for grouse on a beautiful fall day when he and his black lab had narrowly escaped Mike's being attacked by Vern's bear dogs.

The second time it happened, Osborne had asked Vern to take his dogs elsewhere for training: "This is prime grouse territory, and I don't think too many bear hide out in these young aspen. Why don't you take your dogs down the road a bit?" Osborne had spoken politely. At least he thought he had.

The response from Vern was not so polite: "You got a problem with my dogs, asshole, you move down the goddamn road."

But Vern's son, Greg, was not like his old man. A manager in his father's construction company, Greg struck Osborne as a calm, well-spoken young man. "You know Greg Steidl, don't you?" Osborne asked Mallory.

"He was a couple years behind me in high school," said his daughter. "Seemed like a quiet kind of guy. Didn't he play basketball, Dad?"

"I am freezing out here," said Lew before Osborne could answer. "Judith, if you will lead the way. Just tell the family that I stopped you in front of Rudd's home minutes ago and asked where I could find the family members."

"I can do that. Then what would you like me to say?"

"Nothing. I'll take it from there, and Doc and I won't stay any longer than necessary. I need contact information from them and I want to make appointments for interviews with each one. That shouldn't take long."

Osborne and Lew followed the two women up a recently shoveled walkway to the red front door. It had a large brass knocker in the shape of a wild duck in flight. Judith rapped the knocker. The door opened immediately.

"What the—?" said Sloane Tomlinson. She didn't finish her remark but stepped forward so that her bulky frame filled the doorway. "Judith," her tone was accusing, "Kenzie told you this was family only." She peered over Judith's shoulder. "*You* are not welcome, Chief Ferris. This is a private family gathering."

"I understand," said Lew, her voice even. "Judith has nothing to do with Dr. Osborne and myself being here. I have just five minutes of official business with you and your family members. Then we will be happy to leave."

"Oh no, you don't," said a lively voice from behind Sloane. "Come in, come in. I have hot chocolate and donuts."

The woman to whom the voice belonged pushed Sloane to one side as she thrust a hand at Lew. "I'm Kenzie and this is my house. I'm in charge here," she said.

An eager face with a wide toothy grin greeted them with an air of enthusiasm that was hard to resist. In contrast to her older sister, Osborne liked her immediately. "I mean it—all of you come in out of this cold." She opened the door wide and stood beckoning, wispy light brown hair floating around her face.

"Kenzie," said Sloane, warning, "this is not what we've planned. You know that."

"Oh, Sloanie, don't be so mean." Kenzie thrust an elbow in the direction of her sister's plump torso. She's always mean," laughed the young woman. "Hi, I'm Kenzie Steidl and I know Judith, but you are . . . " She stuck her hand out to Mallory.

"I'm Judith's assistant, Mallory Osborne." Mallory stepped past Kenzie into the house.

"Oh, you look so familiar—I know you, you're the dentist. Dr. Osborne."

"Retired dentist," Osborne corrected her as he shook her hand, "but how do you know I'm a dentist? I've been retired several years."

"Doesn't everyone know everyone in Loon Lake?" said Kenzie as she pulled Lew inside. "Seriously, my girlfriends and I always talk about how good-looking you are for an old guy. They see you at McDonald's and I see you buying dog food at the Loon Lake Market."

"D-a-a-d . . . " Mallory had overheard that and gave Osborne a teasing lift of her eyebrows.

"Chief Lewellyn Ferris with the Loon Lake Police," said Lew as Kenzie closed the door behind her. "Dr. Osborne and I have a short piece of business to take care of with you folks, and then we'll leave. I do not want to interrupt your gathering this morning."

"Oh for heaven's sake, you're not interrupting a thing," said Kenzie with a dismissive flick of her right hand. She turned to Judith and, grabbing her by the shoulders, gave her a swift, hard hug. "Oh, Judy, Judy—you must be so devastated and I am so sorry. I loved Rudd—we all did." Tears glistened.

Lew caught Osborne's eye and he knew what she was thinking: Judith's concern that Kenzie was bipolar could be accurate. She was effusive and welcoming one minute, then sad to the point of tears within seconds. Nevertheless, Osborne found her warm and engaging—with none of the rudeness of the woman who had opened the front door.

The living room they walked into was warm and bright, with quilts and colorful framed pictures scattered across the walls. A dining area at one end opened to a kitchen. As they walked into the room, Kenzie reached out her arms to gather up their parkas, insisting, "If you keep those darn things on you'll roast in here.

"Now, I want you to meet everyone and get something warm in your tummies before you leave. Please." The eagerness in her manner reminded Osborne of Mike, who never failed to greet him with happy hops and a furiously wagging tail.

"You two sit down over there," said Kenzie, directing Lew and Osborne to a loveseat covered in a white fabric dotted with huge purple and green flowers.

In the meantime, Judith had walked over to a tall man who was wearing black slacks and a ribbed, grey wool sweater that fit snugly over an impressive potbelly. "Hello, Tim," said Judith. "I am so surprised to see you here. I thought you were spending your winters down on Bonaire."

The man, leaning against the wall with his arms crossed and a studious look on his face, gave a shrug. "Not yet," he said. That was all he volunteered, not even a welcoming smile. Osborne excused his rudeness. The impact of Rudd's unexpected death must have just hit him.

"Tim, please come over and meet Chief Ferris and Dr. Osborne," said Judith, tugging at his sleeve. "Chief Ferris is in charge of the investigation into Rudd's death. She has a few questions for you."

As they walked toward the sofa, Judith beckoned to Lew. "Chief Ferris, this is Tim Tomlinson, Philip's son who lives in Quebec and on the island of Bonaire." Giving Tim a pleasant look as she spoke, Judith said, "Tim's one of the lucky ones who can afford to live north in the summer and down off the coast of Venezuela in the winter, where the temperature is never below seventy. Right, Tim?"

With a grimace, Tim indicated that he did not appreciate her sharing that information. "Just so you know," he said to Lew, ignoring Judith's gracious comment, "I have personal belongings in Rudd's house that I need back—today."

Lew stood up from the sofa and pulled her notebook from the back pocket of her uniform. "Sorry, Mr. Tomlinson," she said, "but no one is to enter the house or remove anything until we have completed our search of the property.

"I'm sure you've heard that the driver of the logging truck is alleging that your stepmother was pushed in front of his truck. So until we know more, I have to consider her death a homicide. That means her home is considered a potential crime scene until my deputies and myself are sure there is no evidence on or around the property."

As she spoke, Tim cocked his head to one side. He seemed to be considering an argument, but he didn't say anything.

Osborne couldn't remember ever seeing the man before. Judith had mentioned that he was close to forty, two years younger than Sloane, but his receding hairline, pale complexion, wire-rimmed glasses, air of reserve, and portly figure made him look older. Older and out of condition. It didn't help that while Lew was asking for his name and contact information, he held his nose high as if something nearby smelled bad.

"As part of our investigation I would like to interview you late this afternoon or tomorrow morning—we have to complete our search of the property first," said Lew.

"Can't do it," said Tim. "The reason I'm here is I'm booked on a flight to Bonaire early tomorrow morning—a flight out of Minneapolis. I'm leaving here to drive to the cities shortly. Sorry."

"Well," said Lew, choosing her words with care. "We'll have to work something out because you cannot leave until I say so."

"And why on earth would that be?" said Tim with a bewildered expression on his face. "You can't possibly suspect *me* of pushing that woman in front of the truck."

Osborne did not miss the tone in which he said "that woman." It would not be necessary to ask Tim how he felt about his stepmother.

"I didn't say that," said Lew. "But one or more of her family members—and I'm including Judith Fordham in this group, too—may have important information that can help us find the person or persons behind her death. Information you may not be aware that you have."

"What a time waste," said Tim, nose sniffing at the air again. "This is the silliest thing I've heard of."

"Rudd wasn't *pushed*," said Sloane from across the room, her voice loud and grating. "She slipped on the ice and fell. You know damn well that driver is just trying to cover his ass. You are forcing us into the most absurd—"

Tim turned toward his sister. "Sloane, shut up." Anger flashed across Sloane's face, but she stayed silent, eyes smoldering.

"Mr. Tomlinson," said Lew, her pen poised over the notebook, "tell me what you do, please. What kind of work? And is your full name Tim or Timothy?"

"Tim. Just Tim." Crossing his arms and rocking back and forth on the soles of his feet, he said in a tone implying terminal boredom: "I do three things for which I do not get paid . . . yet."

He proceeded to speak in a tone so deliberate that he implied his audience was too stupid to understand him otherwise: "Thanks to the modest inheritance I received after my mother's death, I am able to work independently as an artist. I am also an expert scuba diver and an amateur geologist, which is why I winter in Bonaire. I do abstract acrylic paintings of the sea creatures that live in the water down there. My work is very, oh, David Hockney-ish, if you must. But I doubt you know who I am talking about."

"You're right about that," said Lew lightly. She gave a brisk smile as she said, "Now, Mr. Tomlinson, since neither you nor either of your sisters will be able to leave Loon Lake until I've completed my interrogations of each of you, I suggest you change your flight."

"*Interrogations?* You make it sound like we're criminals," said Tim with a condescending smile. Lew ignored the comment.

"What about Greg? Don't you need to talk to him?" asked Kenzie, walking in from the kitchen with a tray holding a coffee carafe, cups, saucers, and a plate of donuts. As uncomfortable as Osborne felt in the current company, the donuts looked appetizing. She tipped her head back toward the kitchen where two men had just appeared in the doorway.

"Greg," said Kenzie as she lowered the tray onto the coffee table, "I want you to come meet Chief Ferris."

Greg Steidl was a younger, healthier version of his father, who remained in the doorway chewing on a toothpick. He appeared hesitant to join the group. Vern Steidl was a tall, wide-shouldered man whose broad chest and narrow hips were emphasized by the white button-down shirt tucked into the belt at his waistline. In his black leather jacket and crisply pressed Levi's, Vern held himself with the self-important air of a man convinced he was attractive to women—but his was a physique that Osborne had learned to associate with the risk of an early heart attack.

His son, on the other hand, was just as tall but as slim as a marathon runner. While the older man's features, bulbous under a shock of white hair combed forward and emphasized by a trim white beard and wire-rimmed glasses, testified to a taste for red meat and hard liquor, the son could not have been more clean-cut. He wore his dark brown hair in a sedate crew cut and only a slight crook of his nose, identical to Vern's, hinted of his parentage.

"Pleased to meet you, Chief Ferris," said Greg, shaking Lew's hand. "I really hope I can help with your investigation. Rudd was a kind, generous woman, always good to Kenzie and me. We were shocked when we heard the news." As he spoke, he slipped his arm around his wife's waist. Osborne was struck by how young the two of them seemed.

"I appreciate that," said Lew. Turning toward the man standing in the doorway, she said, "And you must be Vern, Greg's father." Flipping to a new page in her notebook, pen in hand, she walked over to Vern. "Address, please? Phone numbers?"

She jotted his answers down, then looked up at Vern. She was about to speak when he said, "Cut the crap, Ferris. You've got all the information on me you need. One of your officers with nothing better to do cited me for driving without a seat belt just last month." Vern shook his head. "Worse than a game warden, that idiot."

Osborne smiled to himself. Vern might pride himself on his male superiority around women, but he had just picked on the wrong one. The man's idiocy knew no bounds.

"That's not why I'm here this morning," said Lew, her voice stern. "If you have a problem with anyone in my department, Vern, I suggest you share it with the mayor. But before you do, I suggest you keep in mind that seat belt violations are against the law. I do recall your citation and I also recall that Officer

Adamczak's citation was a warning with no fine attached. You have a problem with that?"

Anger flashed in Vern's eyes before he said in a restrained voice, "Okay, yes, Greg is my son. I run Steidl Builders and Greg is my CFO—he handles the purchasing and billing for our construction projects. We build commercial—"

Before he could say another word, Kenzie piped up: "Yeah, but before that Vern was the caretaker for my dad—all the buildings, the docks, and boats. Mom's place, too. That's how Greg and I met. We used to play together in the big house while Vern was working. We were five years old then—and today is our third wedding anniversary." She beamed.

That explains why Kenzie is so happy and outgoing, thought Osborne. He had been wondering, given the grim reason for the family meeting, why she, of the three Tomlinson siblings, was so upbeat.

"Honey, that's not why they're here," said Greg, squeezing her waist. "Sorry," he looked at Lew, "my wife's been a little carried away today . . . "

"Kenzie," said Vern, his voice thundering across the room. "Have you forgotten your meds again?"

"N-o-o." Kenzie sounded flustered. She threw a worried look at her husband. "Why? I feel fine."

"Dad," said Greg, "Dr. O'Hearne has her tapering off—oh, sweetie. Don't cry." Greg reached over to hug Kenzie around the shoulders. He glared at his father. "Mind your own business for once, will you?"

Vern shrugged off his son's dismay. Osborne saw him wink in Tim's direction.

"Now, now," said Judith, jumping up from where she had been sitting, in the corner with Mallory. "Let's get on with our plans for a memorial for Rudd.

"And, by the way, Greg and Vern—I'd like you two to meet Mallory Osborne. Rudd and I hired her to be the marketing director for the Tomlinson Museum, so she will be my right-hand person and she'll be able to answer any questions you may have in the future."

"I remember you from high school," said Greg, walking over to shake Mallory's hand.

"Osborne? You related to the old man here?" asked Vern, leaving the doorway to take a nearby chair.

"Yes, I'm Dr. Osborne's daughter—"

"Doc Osborne's your old man, huh. Say, Doc, still got that wild hair up your ass against bear hunters? And what the hell brings *you* out this way anyhoo? No one here needs a traveling dentist that I can see." Vern chortled at his own joke.

"Vern, I'm afraid you've been out of the loop. I retired from my practice over two years ago." Osborne kept his voice even while wondering where this conversation was going. It was becoming clear that Vern had been drinking.

"Dr. Osborne is an expert in dental forensics," said Lew, interrupting the conversation, "and he has been deputized on several occasions to help out the Loon Lake Police when we've needed expertise in homicide investigations. The Wausau Crime Lab can't afford a full-time odontologist, and dental records are still the best way to identify dead bodies. Plus, as you may know, our coroner has had some, um . . . health issues, so Dr. Osborne takes over when necessary."

"Good, that's cleared up," said Judith with a withering look at Vern. "If no one else has a question for Dr. Osborne or Chief Ferris, I would like to share with everyone my idea for a memorial gathering. I think we should tie it into an announcement about the founding of the Tomlinson Museum—"

"Whoa, Nellie," said Vern. "Doesn't all that money and land that Rudd inherited from Philip go back to his family now?" Vern glanced around the room, which was silent.

"I mean, doesn't it? You know, years ago, right after Caroline's death, Philip and I had a handshake deal that I could buy a couple lots from him, over in the field, and it's pissed me off ever since that he forgot about our deal. I planned to use those acres for deer hunting and I'd sure as hell like someone to follow through on that."

"As executor of my friend's estate, I'll be happy to check into that, Vern. I assume you have some paperwork? But let me finish, okay?"

Meanwhile, Lew had returned to her seat on the sofa and held out her notebook so Osborne could see a short note she had written: "Unless they make us leave, I want to stay right here."

Osborne gave a slight nod. He couldn't agree more.

Chapter Thirteen

"What I want to discuss with all of you," said Judith, her voice calm, "is that, yes, Rudd named me executor of her estate, but she also established a trust that specifies how her assets will be used and the land is part of that." She glanced at Vern as she spoke.

"Twenty million dollars will go to building the museum in the big field next to her home. The architectural plans were completed last month. Forty million will go toward the purchase of the art—paintings, drawings, and studies by two female artists whom she and Philip chose before his death: Georgia O'Keeffe and Helen Frankenthaler.

"What about the Monet, the Corot, and all the other art that she and my dad owned? Those are worth millions," said Tim. "Can we have those?"

"If you mean the Corot that Sloane tried to take, the answer is no. Rudd was in the process of selling those, with the money used to establish an endowment to pay operating costs for the museum over the coming years."

"I was worried that someone would try to steal it," said Sloane, defending herself. "I mean, with no one in the house, those paintings are not safe. They are too valuable."

"They're reproductions," said Judith in a blunt tone. "Right after Philip's death, Rudd had the Monet, the Corot, and several more of the most valuable paintings copied. They look like the real thing, but they aren't."

"Why would she do that?" asked Sloane, visibly upset.

"Living alone this far out in the country, she told me she felt vulnerable. Twice she found evidence that someone had tried to enter the house when she wasn't home. At the time, the security system worked, but she knew that it wasn't infallible, so she decided to take the precaution of having replicas made and storing the original artworks in a facility over in the cities that specializes in storage for fine art and antiques."

"Do we know where that is?" asked Tim.

"I do and no one else, with the exception of one of her lawyers. Now here's something no one here knows. Two months ago, Rudd learned that her cancer had recurred—aggressively. The doctors gave her less than six months. So she made the decision to return the money not needed for the museum to Philip's adult children and their heirs—all of you here this morning. As executor of her will, I am to oversee that."

"And how much are we talking about?" asked Tim. Osborne marveled at how Tim could ask a reasonable question but make it sound like a putdown of his stepmother and her friend.

Judith looked around the room as she said, "Approximately fifty to sixty million dollars." She paused. "The good news for all of you is that her lawyers have drawn up the paperwork for that to happen. The bad news is she died before she could sign those papers."

"Oh, my God," said Sloane. No one else said a word. Osborne saw Vern toss his toothpick onto the floor as he mouthed an epithet.

"I have every reason to believe that I can sign those papers on her behalf," said Judith. "But I am not signing anything until we know who pushed Rudd in front of that logging truck."

"And if you don't sign, what happens?" asked Tim.

"The entire trust—investments and land assets—goes to the museum under the original plan. The family won't get a dime."

"Wow," said Kenzie, "how do we make that happen—find out who pushed Rudd, I mean?"

"Hey," said Vern from across the room, "leave it to rocket scientist Kenzie to ask the big question. How the hell do you think they find out, dumbyak? They *investigate*. Chief Ferris, here, *investigates*. Her team is great on seat belts—let's sit tight and see what she can do with an obvious accident. Let's see how much time can be wasted on an *investigation*." Vern threw his arms into the air as he said, "We all know Sloane is right: This entire brouhaha is all about a truck driver covering his ass. That's it, plain and simple." With an authoritative thrust of his chin, Vern stood with his feet apart and arms crossed, challenging anyone to contradict him.

Judith shrugged him off as if he were a mosquito.

"To answer Kenzie's very good question," she said, "we start by cooperating with Chief Ferris." She looked over at Tim. "Which means you now have every reason to change those flights."

Ignoring her comment, Tim turned on his heel and started for the kitchen. Midway, he paused in front of one of the armchairs to stare down at Kenzie, who hunched her shoulders, cowering as she avoided his eyes. Without a word, Tim continued into the kitchen, with Vern following behind him.

Osborne knew he was being unkind, unfair, and unprofessional, but two words popped into his mind every time he looked at Tim Tomlinson: *malevolent bastard.*

"Thank you, Judith," said Lew, getting up from the sofa. As she stood up, she bumped Osborne's right elbow, causing him to spill coffee from the cup he had just picked up.

"Uh-oh," said Osborne. "Kenzie, paper towels? Afraid I just spilled coffee on your wood floor."

"Under the sink, Dr. Osborne," said Kenzie, who had walked over to Mallory and Judith as soon as Tim left the room. She was holding an iPad and Osborne heard her say, "Judith, I want to show you something. I posted this great picture of me and Greg from our wedding—it's on Facebook. It's got all our family in it and I've tagged everyone . . . "

While she was talking, Osborne hurried to the kitchen. When he got there, the room was empty. Vern and Tim had stepped outside onto the deck where Vern was having a cigarette. Though their voices were muffled as if they were deliberately keeping them low, he heard Vern say, "Goddammit, Tim, I thought you said your lawyer succeeded in reversing the terms of Philip's trust."

"That's what he told me," said Tim. "Two weeks ago he said it was a done deal, that we'd get it all back."

"Doesn't sound like it this morning."

"Maybe laws in Bonaire are different," said Tim. "Maybe he's still working on it."

"Maybe it's too goddamn late," said Vern, spitting out the words. He threw his cigarette into the snow. As he yanked open the back-porch door, Osborne knelt to search under the sink where he grabbed a roll of paper towels.

The two men walked back into the kitchen, both looking down as they stomped the snow off the their boots. Neither paid attention to Osborne as he stood up with paper towels in hand. "Coffee spill," he said, excusing his presence.

Twenty minutes later, as Osborne, Lew, Judith, and Mallory went to their cars, Lew stopped Judith. "So, you *do* have life insurance, don't you? I've been worried that you might be our next victim."

"Oh, I hadn't thought of that . . . Yes, I see what you mean. Since I've known for weeks now that Rudd's money would go to the museum, I never thought anyone would think that *I* was her heir. Pretty weird assumption if you ask me.

"But now the entire family has an incentive to cooperate with your investigation, so who knows what will surface. I couldn't mention anything about the trust last night because I didn't know for sure that as executor I would have the authority to sign it over. Then early this morning I had a call from the lawyer with the trust division. He gave me that assurance."

"Judith, Doc and I are going over to the house right now. I have Bruce Peters from the crime lab due to meet us there. My hope is that we can finish our investigation of the property and the main house by late today. I know you would appreciate being able to work from there. It shouldn't take too long."

Minutes later, as he climbed into Lew's cruiser, Osborne said, "I heard something interesting when I went into the kitchen to get paper towels, Lew."

"The whole morning was interesting," said Lew as she turned the ignition, then looked over at him while the engine warmed up. "Doc, what do you call a cluster of spiders? A coven?"

"That's witches."

"Close enough," she shrugged. "What a crew. So, Doc, what did you hear?"

"Tim and Vern were having a cigarette out on the back porch and Vern was upset," said Osborne.

"Vern? If anyone should be upset it's his daughter-in-law. That rude remark of his to Kenzie was uncalled for. Poor girl."

"Vern accused Tim of lying about the estate. Apparently Tim had told him that he'd hired a lawyer who could challenge the terms of Rudd's inheritance and return the entire Tomlinson estate—money and land—to the family. Until this morning, Vern thought that was the case. But either Tim never got the bad news from his lawyer or he neglected to tell Vern that it wasn't going to happen."

Lew snorted. "What's the old joke? Have you ever heard a lawyer say they couldn't win a case?"

Osborne chuckled as she pulled onto the road heading back toward Rudd's home.

"Still, that's very interesting, Doc. Vern and Tim, huh. Makes you wonder what they're up to."

Glancing into her rearview mirror, Lew saw a black Jeep following her cruiser. It looked like one of the cars that had been parked in front of Kenzie and Greg's home when they had arrived earlier. But Loon Lake had a lot of black Jeeps, so she didn't think twice about it.

As Lew punched the code to the gate at Rudd's driveway, her cell phone rang. Raising it to her ear, a sudden movement in the rearview mirror caught her eye. The Jeep had pulled in right behind her. Tim Tomlinson was behind the wheel.

"Yes, Todd?" Her cell phone to her ear, Lew turned off the ignition and waited.

"Chief, we got an ice fisherman missing. I've called in the county dive-rescue team, but I think you need to know who it is—Chip Dietz."

"Uh-oh," said Lew. "Todd, Doc Osborne is right here with me. I'm putting you on speaker."

"Sure," said the officer.

"You mean that young kid who washes dishes at the Grizzly Bear Café?"

"His mom reported him missing late last night when he didn't come home from fishing. She said he fishes every night after work, but he likes to be home by nine o'clock. She didn't call dispatch until this morning, kept hoping he'd spent the night at his girlfriend's, but when he didn't show up for work—"

"Hold on, Todd, I've got someone waving at me here."

After motioning for Osborne to stay in the car, Lew opened her door and said, "Mr. Tomlinson, hold on a minute, will you? I'm dealing with an emergency." She closed the door before saying, "Okay, Todd. So the dive rescue guys are working this?"

"Yes. I'm here with them on Moen Lake—over by the big boulder with the flag marker—you know, the spot where everyone fishes off the sandbar. No sign of the kid, but all his gear is here. We're pretty sure he fell in."

"Fell?"

"Yeah, slipped on the ice maybe?"

Osborne saw doubt cross Lew's face. He shook his head. This did not sound good.

"I'll call the minute I know more," said Todd.

"Probably too late with all the divers there, but do your best to secure the area, will you? I don't think for a minute that the kid fell in."

"Gotcha, Chief."

Lew closed her phone and stared straight ahead as she said, "How is it that the only witness who saw someone who may have pushed Rudd Tomlinson has just disappeared? When was the last time an ice fisherman fell through the ice, Doc?"

Osborne and Lew got out of the car. "All right, Tim. What is your problem, because we have work to do here before I have time for you—"

"That's not why I'm here," said Tim, shivering in his sweater as he gestured toward the winged entry to the Tomlinson house. He had left Kenzie's house without pulling on a jacket.

"I have a box in there. It would have been delivered two days ago and it has all my recent paintings. I need it for my trip so I'll just run in and pick it up—"

"No," said Lew. "I thought I made it clear that nothing leaves this house until it has been thoroughly searched. That includes garbage and mail. I have your cell number and I will call you when we're done."

She turned to walk toward the entrance, with Tim following like an anxious dog. "But it's *my* box." It had been a long time since Osborne had seen a grown man about to cry.

"Is it addressed to you?"

"No, but Rudd knew I was sending it in her care. She said the museum might have a gift shop and she would consider carrying my paintings in the shop. Now I need to pack those for my trip."

While Tim was talking, two vehicles entered through the open gate and pulled into the driveway beside Lew's cruiser: Ray's battered blue pickup with its rusty winter topper on it and Bruce Peters's white SUV with Wausau Crime Lab lettered along the sides.

"Hold on, Ray," said Lew as Ray jumped from the pickup and hurried toward where Lew and Osborne were standing. "Taking care of an issue here. Do you know Tim Tomlinson?" She gestured toward the shivering man.

"Yo, man," said Ray, "haven't seen you since my dad and I went fishing with you and your old man back in the day. How's it goin'?" Tim shrugged off the question with a fierce look at Lew.

"Now, Tim, since I've recommended that you change your flight—getting the box back later shouldn't be a problem."

Tim's face reddened. He turned and started back to the Jeep, slipping sideways on the icy surface. Reaching to open the car door, he paused and turned around. "Something you should know, Chief Ferris. Kenzie pushed our mother down the stairs—that was no accident."

Lew studied the man's face for a long moment before she said, "Thank you, Tim. I'll check the police report on your mother's accident. I wasn't on the force then, but I'm sure our former chief conducted a comprehensive investigation."

"You won't find it in the report. Kenzie was the only one in the house when Mother fell. And she lied. She's always lied. She's schizophrenic, you know. She does weird stuff. Always has."

"We'll discuss that later. Right now Dr. Osborne and I have official business to take of, so *please*—go back to your family."

"Hey, now," said Ray, watching as Tim spun the tires on the Jeep. "There's a guy looks like he strangles deer." Lew shook her head and unlocked the front entry to the house.

Chapter Fourteen

Over the next three hours, Bruce took sets of fingerprints throughout the house as well as photographs of the interior—rooms, shelves, closets, and the kitchen cabinets. The fingerprints would be analyzed to see if there were any that did not match people, like Rudd Tomlinson, who were expected to be in the house on a regular basis.

During that time, Ray explored the property right around the house, checking for any signs of attempted entry or unusual patterns of footprints. He also shot photos of the interior of the four-car garage and lawn storage shed.

Starting on the second level, Lew and Osborne went through Rudd's personal belongings as well as all the contents of the master bedroom and bath, the three unused guest bedrooms, the library, a den that was used as an office, and the kitchen and living room areas. They kept an eye out for anything that seemed out of place, especially in Rudd's office.

"Well, so much for that," said Lew as the afternoon wound down. "If there is anything to be found we don't seem able to do so."

All that remained to be searched at that point was the large, four-foot-by-four-foot cardboard box that was so important to Tim. With help from Osborne, Lew sliced open the box, pulled the flaps back, and peered in. She could see what appeared to be picture frames protected with Bubble Wrap and neatly stacked side by side.

"Before we pull these out, I'd like to have Judith take a look," said Lew. "Since she's familiar with the plans for the museum, she may know Rudd's reason for having Tim ship his paintings to her. It doesn't sound right to me."

"And he's so worried about it," said Osborne.

Twenty minutes later, Judith and Mallory walked into the foyer of the house just as Ray and Bruce finished their searches.

"Ah, if it isn't my Picture Lady," said Ray with one of his most engaging grins. Uh-oh, thought Osborne, who had watched more than one intelligent woman, Mallory included, succumb to Ray's charm. He knew what was coming next . . .

Sure enough, Ray curled the upper-right corner of his lip and let go with a soft trill ending in 'tyeep.' Judith blushed. Mallory rolled her eyes.

"I know that one—spring robin!" said Bruce, bushy eyebrows bouncing with delight. Bruce might have been masterful at scouting crime scenes, but the tall man with the hyper eyebrows, full head of curly black hair, and black moustache to match, was a kindergartner at heart.

Osborne swore there were two reasons Lew could always lure Bruce north to help with an investigation: one, he wanted her expert advice on his casting; two, he could never get over how a man wearing a fish on his head could get hired as a deputy by the Loon Lake Police. Bruce also knew not to ask too many questions.

For Lew, giving advice to a budding and overly enthusiastic fly-fisherman was a welcome relief from dealing with his superiors. "Dear Lord, please spare me those Wausau boys" had been her lament before Bruce joined the crime lab. The director had openly sneered when Lew was promoted to chief.

"Women do not belong in combat or on patrol," the jerk had said to Lew's face the first time she had to work with him. "I'll do what I have to for your officers, but don't expect me to excuse your mistakes, Lewellyn."

To this day, Lew was sure he was chagrined that she had not made any awful "mistakes." And he had no clue as to how she succeeded in snagging Bruce to help on her cases. The answer was easy: fly-fishing. As long as she supplied Bruce with insight and casting tips, his cooperation was guaranteed. Not even winter with its hard water got in the way, as Bruce was learning to tie his own trout flies, and again he needed the same advice from Lew that an aspiring cook needs from a blue-ribbon chef. Today would be no different.

"Chief Ferris, before we check that box, can I show you something?" asked Bruce, beckoning them all into the living-room area. He walked over to the tall case holding the fly rods and pointed to a framed set of colorful trout flies. "What are those?"

"Oh, do you mind if I answer him?" asked Judith, stepping in front of Lew.

"Bruce," said Lew, "this is Judith Fordham. She was the victim's closest friend and is the executor of her estate. They fly-fished together."

"You gotta be kidding me," said Bruce, his eyebrows hitting the ceiling. "You fly-fish?"

Lew held her breath, hoping Bruce would not say something politically incorrect. There was a fierce intelligence about Judith that implied she would not suffer any cracks about women fishing.

"We did," said Judith. "What you are looking at are trout flies that were tied by one of our instructors when we were at the Wulff School of Fly Fishing. We called them Rapunzels, but I think the official name is a Wilcox Rapunzel Olive. Aren't they beautiful? Too gorgeous to lose to a fish. That's why Rudd had them framed."

As Bruce leaned in for a closer look, she said, "Fly-fishermen call the Rapunzel 'a dragon of a nymph.' It's a Size 12 and tied to look like a damselfly. Great for nymph fishing, but Rudd and I never risked losing one. We always used a Royal Wulff since each of us owned dozens of those—and we did best with dry flies."

"Chief," Bruce gave Lew a questioning look, "any chance you can teach me how to tie one of these Rapunzels?"

"Not sure. I'll have to check my dead animal room," said Lew, referring to the corner of her farmhouse where she kept her fly tying supplies. "I'll check tonight and see what I got."

"Do you mind if I check out these rods?" asked Bruce. "I've taken prints off the cabinet and I'll keep my nitrile gloves on."

"Judith?" asked Lew. "Do you mind?"

"Go right ahead. That Joan Wulff Winston was Rudd's favorite. It's a honey."

"Say, Mallory, you back home for good?" asked Ray while Bruce explored the contents of the rod cabinet.

"Not sure," said Mallory, with a brief explanation of her new position with the Tomlinson Museum. "If everything works the way Judith and I hope it will, I'll be around for at least a year."

"Good," said Ray. He put an arm around Mallory's shoulders and gave her a friendly squeeze. She smiled back. Osborne glanced away, relieved to see only friendship between the two.

His eldest daughter and his neighbor were two of his favorite people, but their brief romance two years ago had alarmed Osborne. Mallory, just out of her marriage to a man Osborne had detested, was on an emotional roller coaster at the time. And while Ray was one of Osborne's closest friends, he was not someone Osborne needed to have as a son-in-law. That prospect had been unnerving.

"Ladies," said Ray when Bruce closed the door to the rod cabinet, "Bruce baby here . . . has twisted my arm . . . " Ray paused as he raised his right index finger, which was the signal that he was about to deliver life-changing information, "to find a couple of waxies and take him ice fishing in the morning. Judith, have you thought it over—interested in going along?"

"I've never done that," said Judith. "Sounds fascinating. I'm in."

"Mallory?" asked Ray.

"No, thank you. I am not a fan of freezing to death. Judith, you go right ahead."

"Oh, but like I said at the pub," Judith's face fell, "I don't have the right clothes."

"Yes, you do," said Mallory. "I'll lend you my snowmobile gear—pants, jacket, boots, gloves—"

"And I've got a hat you can borrow," said Ray.

"I'll bet you do," said Judith, her laugh pealing through the room. It was the happiest Osborne had seen her since she had arrived. "What's a waxie? Do I need to get one of those, too?"

"It's a white worm that Ray carries in his cheek," said Mallory. "Disgusting."

"Maybe, but effective," said Ray. "Walleyes love 'em."

"All right, attention, everyone," said Lew. "Now that you've got all your extracurricular activities in order, please help me with the contents of that box that's out in the foyer—the one Tim sent."

As they walked into the foyer, headlights flashed in the driveway and the outside lights showed a small red sedan pulling in to park behind Ray's pickup. In less than a minute a figure appeared in the glass doorway: Kenzie Steidl.

She was carrying a large covered casserole dish in mittened hands. She backed off as Lew opened the door, saying, "I know the house is still off-limits, but I made wild rice soup for later. It'll keep in the fridge—"

"No, you can come in, Kenzie. We're about finished here," said Lew.

Chapter Fifteen

The sky outside the windowed foyer was darkening as Bruce and Ray helped Lew pull the large, heavy, wrapped rectangles from the box. Judith took the first one over to the small oak bench in the corner, sat down, and started to unwrap it.

As she pulled off the first layer of Bubble Wrap, she looked down at a painting of a barracuda. "What? What was Rudd thinking?"

Looking over her shoulder, Mallory said, "Well . . . it *is* a fish . . . "

"Not one you see in Wisconsin," said Judith. "What the hell is Tim up to?"

"Maybe he just wanted her opinion on his work." Mallory's tone was conciliatory.

"That's not what he told Chief Ferris," said Judith as she tore down corners of the wrapping of the second and third paintings. She held the second painting out in front of her. "Okay, now we have a family of goats. Great." She picked up the third framed painting. "And a coral reef. Colorful, yes, but not right for the Tomlinson Museum. All right, let's take a look at the last three . . . "

Judith sighed as she started to remove the wrapping from the fourth painting. She stopped. She stared at the canvas, then ripped off the remaining Bubble Wrap. No fish this time. The painting was of a naked woman, bound and twisted and with streaks of black blood across her body. A small picture of Rudd's face, which appeared to have been clipped from a larger photo, was stuck in one corner between the canvas and the frame. It resembled the face of the woman in the painting.

"Oh, my God," said Judith, gasping. Everyone in the room was silent.

She reached for the fifth painting. This time, the figure was a naked child with demon eyes and hands stained black. Again a small black-and-white photo of Rudd's face was stuck up in the corner. The last painting showed a woman's head, deathly white, smashed face-down against a blood-red surface. No photo attached.

Judith looked up at Lew, who had walked over to stand beside her. "Was Tim sending a message?"

"He hurt her, too," whispered Kenzie. She was standing beside Mallory, close enough to get a good view of the paintings.

"What?" Lew turned to the young woman. "What did you just say?"

But Kenzie, still in her winter jacket, raced for the sliding glass doors leading out of the foyer. She ran down the driveway, but before reaching the road she jumped over the snow bank and disappeared into the dark woods.

Everyone in the room stood still, astonished. Then Ray was out the door after her. Plunging through the snow, he shouted, "Kenzie, stop!" She kept going, staggering thorough the pines, sobbing. Tackling her from behind, Ray brought Kenzie down face-first into the snow.

Lew and Bruce came running up from behind. "Are you okay?" asked Lew, helping her to her feet and brushing the snow from her teary face. "You're hysterical, Kenzie. No one's going to hurt you. Take a deep breath. Another one. Good." Arm around the girl's shoulders, Lew led her back toward the house.

She escorted Kenzie to one of the sofas in the living room where she had her sit down, take off her jacket, and have a drink of water. Judith, Mallory, Osborne, Ray, and Bruce stood near the back of the room, leaving the two women together.

After a few minutes, Kenzie laid her head on Lew's shoulder. "Does Tim hurt you?" asked Lew, her voice kind.

"He did. I was six years old when he did it the first time. Then he drew pictures and made me look—pictures like that child with the bloody hands and no clothes. That was me." She lifted sad eyes to Lew.

"When did it stop?"

"The day Greg caught him. We were like ten years old. Greg beat him up. He told Tim he'd kill him if he did it again. So he stopped, but he's always been mean."

"Did you tell anyone what he was doing?"

"I tried." Kenzie sniffed. "Sloane told me I was lying."

"What about your mother? Did you tell her?"

"I tried, but she said I was making it up." Kenzie took a deep breath. "Mother never liked me. Once she told me I shouldn't have been born, I was an accident, and just looking at me made her mad. I mean, I know why. I've never been pretty like Sloane or . . . cool like Tim."

Lew dropped her head, thinking over Kenzie's remarks. She looked up. "Kenzie, I have to ask you a couple more questions because I need to understand the dynamics of your family."

"And when you do that, will you let me know?" asked Judith in a wry tone from where she'd sat down on a stool at the kitchen island. Lew waved for her not to talk.

"Did Tim's hurting you involve sex?"

Kenzie nodded with her eyes closed. "He bullied me into it."

"I see. Where is he right now? At Sloane's?"

"Maybe. I'm not sure. Sometimes he stays at Vern's place."

"And Greg's mother? Is she there, too?"

"No. They've been divorced for years. She lives in Milwaukee. She wants nothing to do with Vern. Greg and I spend Christmas with her."

"Do your husband and his father get along?"

"Vern pays Greg well. Greg is really good with numbers, so Vern doesn't bother him. He needs Greg for the business.

"See, when Dad's cancer came back, we thought that when he died I would inherit a lot of money and Greg could start his own business. That was two years ago and we were wrong. It's hard to make a decent living up here, so Greg really has to work for his dad. Especially if we want to have a family."

She pushed tears away from her cheeks and looked over at Judith. "If they don't find who pushed Rudd, then all the money goes to the museum, doesn't it?"

"Afraid so," said Judith. "Kenzie, Rudd told me she helped you get professional counseling. Is that working okay?"

"I think so," said Kenzie. "I have a good therapist. She says I'm bipolar, so I take meds for that. Sorry about running off. Those pictures are just so . . . evil. They scare me."

"Have you told your therapist about Tim?"

"Um, no. You're the first people I've told except for Greg." Kenzie looked around the room with fearful eyes. "You won't tell anyone, will you? I'm afraid what Tim might do if he found out. He told me he would kill me if I ever told anyone. I . . . I know he would, too. I had a baby bird once. He killed it."

"Tell me if he touches you, kid," said Ray. "I'll beat the crap out of him."

"Ray," said Lew with a warning glance. "Stay out of it."

"Please, don't make it worse," said Kenzie. "Greg says he can't hurt me. But whenever he's around, my stomach feels awful. I keep waiting for him to do something."

"Chief Ferris," said Judith, "he scares me, too. I can't have those paintings here in the house."

"I'll take them to the station," said Lew. Her cell phone rang. She answered, listened, and said, "We'll be there in twenty minutes, Todd."

Chapter Sixteen

The floodlights set up around the holes in the ice where the divers had gone through made the scene on the snow-covered lake bright as day. Black-hooded figures in dry suits and tanks could be seen pulling themselves up from the water like aliens breaking through from the depths below.

With Bruce and Ray following in their vehicles, Lew and Osborne drove across the ice on the snowmobile trail. As they neared the site, they could see Lew's officers, Donovan and Adam-czak, huddled near the van belonging to the dive-rescue team along with another man who turned out to be a detective from the sheriff's department. A body in sodden clothing lay face up on a cot at their feet.

"Chief, I'm afraid we've made a mess of the site," said Todd Donovan, gesturing at all the footprints in the snow and slush, as Lew walked up. "No other way for the divers to go in. It took them an hour to locate the victim as it was. The water in this lake is so dark with tannin that it's hard to see in the summertime, much less when three feet of ice filters the light."

"I understand. Not much you can do about that," said Lew. "Have you spoken with the family?"

"His mother is meeting us at the morgue," said Todd. "She's a widow and doesn't get around real easy. I didn't want her out here."

"I'll go with you," said Lew. "Let's step back and let Doc take care of official business before we all freeze to death."

Opening the black bag that held his instruments and a clipboard with the documents necessary to declare an official cause of death, Osborne knelt over the body of the young man. The snowmobile parka was zipped up to the neck leaving only his head exposed.

With gentle fingers, Osborne tipped the boy's head to one side. "I don't need to tell anyone this victim did not drown."

He glanced up at Lew. "You may want to consider how much his mother has to see when she meets you at the morgue." Osborne pried open what was left of the boy's right jaw—several teeth were shattered. The left side of his head was caved in.

"What do you think happened, Doc?" asked Bruce. "I'll have the body sent down to the lab for an official autopsy first thing in the morning, but your thoughts?"

"Someone used a baseball bat, maybe a sledgehammer," said Osborne. "One blow to knock him out. Then a few more to finish the job."

"Maybe it was this," said Ray, holding up a damaged ice auger, which lay on the snow by a toboggan holding gear.

"Poor kid." Lew clapped her mitts together to keep warm. "Let's secure a wider area here. Check it out first thing in the morning. Might find something."

"I doubt it," said Todd. "Looked to me like he pulled his sled with his gear out along the snowmobile trail over there, and walked here to his usual fishing holes. Enough snow is packed down to make me think he fished here often."

Ray had been walking in a circle around the four holes that had been cut in the ice. He bent down to pick something up. "Any of your boys smoke?" he asked the detective from the dive team. "No, and certainly not tonight," said the man. Ray turned to Todd and Roger with a questioning look.

"No," said both in unison.

Ray extended his deerskin mitt. Two cigarette butts lay in his palm. "Bruce, let's check these against the ones I gave you earlier—the ones I found near where the car had been parked by the Grizzly Bear Café."

"Will do," said Bruce.

"Lew, if you don't need me at the morgue, I'd like Bruce to drive me back to Kenzie and Greg Steidl's home," said Osborne. "That conversation I overheard between Tim and Vern? I was watching out the kitchen window just as Vern tossed a cigarette into the snow. I think we should try to find that."

"You'll need an excuse."

"I'll say I stepped onto the porch to make a call on my cell phone and my car charger fell out of my jacket pocket."

Greg and Kenzie were mildly surprised to have Osborne and Bruce at their door but happy to let them check the back porch and yard. "I've lost two chargers myself," said Greg with a sympathetic smile.

The cigarette butt was right where Vern had tossed it. Osborne stood by while Bruce picked it up and slipped it into an evidence bag.

At six the next morning, Osborne walked into McDonald's to have his third cup of coffee. "Hey, youse guys," he said with a cheery wave to his buddies. "Missed me?"

A round of good-humored putdowns answered him. Sitting down, he was quizzed about the Tomlinson case, but Osborne demurred, saying, "I know what you know from the paper, fellas. We know that Rudd Tomlinson was run over by a logging truck, and the driver insists he saw someone push her. But we have no idea who that might be."

He didn't say anything about Chip Dietz. That would be Lew's call. He had to wait and see what she would decide to tell the local reporters. At this point, the kid's death had not been on the news. He did decide to share that he had met the Tomlinson family.

"I didn't realize that one of the daughters was married to Greg Steidl," said Osborne. "He seems like a nice guy."

"In spite of his old man?" asked Denny Zaremski, a retired insurance agent with whom Osborne had often fished muskie.

"What you mean by that?" asked Osborne, curious to see who shared his negative opinion of the man.

"I probably had three, maybe four, occasions when Vern alleged someone had stolen property off one of his construction sites. He wanted insurance to cover the loss. The second time it happened, I had the company hire a private detective—he found the stolen goods in one of Vern's garages." Denny took a big sip of coffee.

"That's probably the tip of the iceberg when it comes to Vern. Too bad, too, 'cause he had a good thing going with old man Tomlinson years ago."

"You mean Philip?" asked Osborne.

"Yeah. Now I know all this because I wrote the homeowner's and other insurance for Phil Tomlinson. At the time, which was about thirty years ago, he had hired Vern as the caretaker for the estate out there—plus, Phil owned quite a bit of land in the area. He paid Vern well and even sold him six lots out on that pond we call Silver Lake.

"That's how Vern got into the construction business—put up a couple spec homes, made a nice piece of change, and today he's doing okay in spite of himself. That kid of his keeps him on the up and up. In my humble opinion."

"So, what are you implying?" Osborne was used to Denny telling half the story until he was wheedled into revealing the rest: He loved the attention.

"Well now, I shouldn't say anything," said Denny. "When you sell insurance to people you try to assure them that some things will remain confidential. In Phil Tomlinson's case, he was pathological when it came to news concerning his family. He wanted nothing good or bad getting out."

"Hell, one year we hunted together and he got a gorgeous twelve-point buck. Wouldn't even let me take a photo to put up on the wall at the hunting shack. That was a disappointment, I tell you—when was the last time *you* got a twelve-pointer?"

By now all five guys around the table were staring at Denny. Bud Vogel took the bait: "Denny . . . finish your damn story. I gotta pick up the old lady by seven. Get her over to Woodruff for a doctor's appointment. So stop beating around the bush, will you?"

Denny chuckled. "Okay, okay. Vern made the mistake of stealing a really nice Lund fishing boat with a brand-new Mercury outboard from Phil. Just took it one day when he knew Phil was gone, hid it, and tried to say some jabone had broken the lock on the boat lift and stolen it.

"That worked fine until a couple guys out fishing on Boom Lake in Rhinelander spotted Phil's kid, Tim, pulling a couple girls on water skis—with that boat. The only reason they recognized it was because one of the guys worked at the marina where Phil had had it serviced. He called Phil to let him know.

"Turns out Vern and the kid were in cahoots and the plan had been to sell the boat and split the difference. But the kid, wanting to impress the girls, had trailered it over to Rhinelander without Vern knowing. Kid wasn't even sixteen at the time. Didn't have a driver's license.

"When Phil found out, he fired Vern. But he never pressed charges. He did not want the attention. Probably thought any news articles would attract more thieves now that they knew how easy it had been for Vern to steal a good-sized boat. But Vern got punished big time anyway.

"He thought he had a deal going with Phil to buy another piece of property, a section of the Tomlinson land that was open field and would have been perfect for commercial development. But that sure wasn't going to happen now. Still, he's survived over the years."

"And now the Tomlinson Museum is going to be built out there," said Osborne. "Good thing Vern never got any of that land. It will be an ideal setting for the museum—and a real boon for our tourism here in Loon Lake."

"Good," said Denny. "Vern builds crap as it is. Pollutes the skyline, doncha know."

The five men nodded in agreement. Satisfaction, good coffee, and great gossip all around.

Chapter Seventeen

An hour later, Osborne knocked on the door to Lew's office. "Hey, Doc, come in and help yourself to coffee," she said. "Got Kenzie Steidl arriving any minute, so I'm glad you're here."

"She's early. It's not even eight o'clock."

"She called Marlaine, who's on dispatch, half an hour ago and asked if we could meet first thing this morning so she can go ice fishing with Ray and Bruce when they take Judith out."

"Oh, that's unexpected, don't you think?"

"I don't know. She strikes me as a gregarious person—unlike her siblings. I told Marlaine to send her in the minute she gets here, so help yourself to a cup of coffee while I finish up my notes from yesterday."

"Lew," said Osborne as he poured a cup, "at McDonald's this morning Denny Zaremski, who handled the Tomlinson insurance on their properties, said Philip had had a serious falling-out with Vern Steidl years ago involving a stolen boat. He never pressed charges because Tim was in on it with Vern, too."

"Really. I've already been thinking it might behoove having Dani check the files for me. Any idea what year that might have been?"

"Tim wasn't sixteen yet because he was caught driving without a license, if that helps."

A knock on the door and Kenzie poked her head in. "Am I too early?" she asked, breathless from the cold.

"No, no, come right in," said Lew, walking toward her. Kenzie slipped off her heavy sheepskin coat and settled down in the chair next to Osborne, who was sitting in front of Lew's desk.

"Coffee?" asked Osborne, ready to stand up and pour her a cup.

"Gosh, no. I already had a full pot," she said with a gurgle that sounded like an attempt at a laugh. "I had to get up really, really early this morning.

"I usually sleep pretty late 'cause of my meds, y'know? So I went to bed early last night just so I could go fishing this morning, but I still needed a lot of coffee to clear my head. They say I'm bipolar, but some days I think I'm really just over-caffeinated."

Again the nervous laugh. She cleared her throat.

"*Are* you bipolar?" asked Lew, her voice sympathetic. "Is that an official diagnosis?"

"Sort of, but there's all kinds of bipolar. At least that's what Dr. O'Hearne says. But . . . I say—*whatever*. If that works for her, fine." She grinned but Lew did not return the smile.

Kenzie dropped the flip tone. "Okay, yes. I'm bipolar and I take medication for it and, contrary to my idiot father-in-law, I don't forget to take my meds. I don't." She was so adamant that Osborne asked, "Does he always talk to you like that?"

"He likes to pick on me, especially in front of people. Always has, but most of the time I just ignore him." Kenzie gave Osborne a sidelong glance. "He knows I know he's not anywhere near as smart as Greg. That makes him mad.

"Here, I brought something," she said leaning down to reach into the large bag that she had been carrying over one shoulder. She pulled out an iPad, opened the case, and turned it on.

"Before you show us anything, I have questions for you," said Lew, looking up from her notepad, reading glasses balanced on her nose. Watching Lew, Osborne couldn't help thinking as he often did that she looked her most attractive when she was serious.

"How frequently did you see your stepmother, Kenzie? And did she ever seem frightened or worried? Especially over the last two weeks?"

"Almost every day. I would stop by for coffee in the morning. See . . . " Kenzie paused to study the tips of her boots before looking up at Lew, "Rudd and I got along." Dropping her chin, she raised her eyebrows and said in a firm voice, "*In spite of Sloane.*

"Sloane hated that I liked her. But I did. She was always nice to me—bought me this coat for Christmas." Kenzie pointed to her sheepskin coat. "Cost over a thousand dollars, you know. She was nice to me and wonderful to my dad—she was so good to him and I loved her for that.

"But, um, frightened? Not that I could see. But I'm not sure. She was so excited about the museum—

"Ohmygosh, I didn't tell you—she wanted me to run the gift shop! That would have been so much fun. She's even had me looking for one-of-a-kind things to buy for the store."

"Like Tim's paintings?" asked Lew.

The eagerness vanished from Kenzie's face. "No. Absolutely not. She never said anything about wanting those stupid paintings of his." She grimaced. "The only person who ever liked Tim's stuff was our mother. She was ridiculous about it. But, then, he was her favorite, you know."

"About your mother. Were you home when she had her accident?"

Osborne, sitting beside her, saw Kenzie clench her fists. She held them tight, pressing down on her knees.

"I was there but I wasn't there. I was asleep. I didn't know a thing until the paramedics came." The answers tumbled out as if rehearsed. Eyes down, Kenzie shook her head once, then again. When she looked up, her face had stiffened. The enthusiasm with which she had entered the room was gone. This was a different person—a sullen, calculating individual.

"If you were asleep, who found her? Who called 911?"

"The cleaning lady. When I heard the sirens is the first I knew something had happened."

"And who was the cleaning lady? Does she live in Loon Lake or nearby?"

"Catherine Schultz. She's dead. Heart attack a couple years ago. She was an older lady. Can we talk about Rudd?" she begged.

"Sure," said Lew. "When were you first aware that her cancer was back?"

Kenzie looked from Lew to Osborne. "I had no idea it was back. She didn't say a word about it to me. But now that I think back over the last month, maybe that's why she didn't seem as happy as she had been.

"That's why I brought my iPad. I want to show you what a sweet, beautiful person she was. I'm showing this to Judith later this morning. It's the best picture ever of Rudd and maybe we can use it for the museum. You know, for brochures and stuff."

Lew got up from her chair and walked around to stand behind Kenzie as she scrolled down the computer screen. "What are we looking at?" As Kenzie's fingers danced on the keys of her tablet, the tension left her face.

A quick knock on the door and Dani opened it a crack. "Chief? Charlene Murphy is here. Mind if we use the computer in the main conference room?"

"Sure, but hold on a moment. I'd like to see Charlene." Lew got up from her chair and walked over to the door as Dani and a young woman stepped into the room. Kenzie, who had turned around to see who was talking, jumped up saying, "Hey, Charlene. What are you doing here?"

"How do you two know each other?" asked Lew, surprised.

"Charlene is dating one of Greg's good friends," said Kenzie. "We're on Facebook together. Seriously, girl, why are you at the police station? A little traffic issue?" she teased. "Seat belt violation or DUI?"

Before Charlene could answer, Lew stepped in. "She's helping Dani with some agricultural information we need," said Lew, anxious to quell Kenzie's curiosity. She wasn't sure that Charlene needed to have people know about her search for her birth mother.

"And Dani? I didn't know you worked here. I thought you were going to be a hairdresser." Osborne could see that Kenzie was oblivious to the fact that none of this was any of her business.

"Hi, Kenzie," said Dani. "I'm switching careers. I just started as an intern for Chief Ferris—"

"Dani is our data wizard," said Lew, interrupting. "All right, you two, go right ahead and use the conference room. We'll talk later, Dani." She shut the door before Kenzie could say another word.

"Are you and Dani friends on Facebook?" asked Lew as she walked back to her desk.

"I think so," said Kenzie. "I'll have to check. I have over a thousand friends, y'know. Dani and I took a class on how to do gel nails at the tech college together. But that was over a year ago. Not sure if I friended her or not. But what the heck, let me show you the best picture ever of Rudd.

"So these are my photos on Facebook," said Kenzie, focused again on her tablet. She had relaxed and her enthusiasm came bubbling back. "Back in October Greg and I had a fun Halloween party, and Rudd came. She had such a good time. See?"

The photos on the page showed a group of people gathered around a table topped with a punch bowl and glass cups, along with bowls of candies and plates of cookies.

"This was so fun," said Kenzie as she scrolled along the photograph. "I made all those cookies. Took me two days, too."

"Great decorations," said Lew. "I see pumpkins and spiders and . . . what are the long ones supposed to be?"

"Severed fingers," said Kenzie in a triumphant tone. "No one had ever seen *those* before."

All of the guests appeared to be wearing costumes and masks except Rudd, who was wearing only black pants, a black sweater, and a happy expression. In the photo that Kenzie had zeroed in on, Rudd was standing with her arms draped across the shoulders of two people as she looked into the camera.

"Now wait . . . I edited that picture so I got just Rudd and not everyone else." Kenzie pulled up another photo. It was a headshot of a cheerful woman, her hair in dark brown waves around her wide Irish face. She was looking into the camera with a generous smile that showcased her even, white teeth. She looked healthy, even radiant.

"She does look happy," said Lew. "That must have been before her cancer came back. But go back to the group photo, would you please?"

"Sure." The photo came up. Lew leaned forward to study the picture. She pointed to the person standing to Rudd's immediate right. It was an old man in wire-rimmed glasses with a receding hairline. What hair he had was wisps of white and grey pushed behind his ears. He was staring at the camera with intensity.

"Who is that man? Can you bring that figure in closer?"

"Oh, that's me," said Kenzie with a chortle. She leaned in as she spread her fingers on the screen to enlarge the image. "Great mask, huh? I found it online. It's made of silicone—and it's the kind that you pull on over your head. Makeup artists use them and they are *so* realistic.

"And really expensive. That one cost me a hundred and fifty bucks, but I looked *so* real. That mask is amazing. I wore it to town on trick-or-treat night and sat on my friend Sarah's porch to help her give out candy. Scared a lot of little kids with that one."

"Any chance I could get a copy of that photo?" asked Lew.

"Sure. Are you on Facebook? I'll friend you, then you can go to my page . . . "

"I'm not and I prefer not to be on Facebook, Kenzie. Sorry."

"That's okay. I'll download it and email it to you."

"I would appreciate that," said Lew. "Oh wait, maybe my intern, Dani, is on Facebook. If so, she can pull it up, right?"

"Hold on, I'll check right now . . . yep, there she is." Kenzie glanced up at Lew with a pleased look on her face.

As she walked back around her desk, Lew said, "Thank you, Kenzie. This is enough for now. I'm sure I'll have questions for you later, but this has been very, very helpful."

"Um," said Kenzie, getting to her feet. "You won't say anything to Tim about my Halloween party, will you? He wasn't invited."

"Was Sloane there?"

"Yeah," said Kenzie with an apologetic shrug. "I had to have her. She lives right next door to us. She and mean old Vern—just 'cause they're family Greg makes me include them. *Every* Christmas, *every* Thanksgiving, *every* Easter, and *every* Halloween." Kenzie rolled her eyes. "Greg's a lot nicer than I am. I hate it when his dad comes. Jeez, he's fifty years old and he hits on my girlfriends—but that's another story."

"Yes, I imagine it is," said Lew with a low chuckle. "You know, Kenzie, we all have a Vern in our families."

"I s'pose. But if we can find out who killed Rudd, then Greg won't have to work for him anymore. *And maybe then I won't have to invite him ever again. Vern or Tim, the creeps.*" She turned off her iPad with vehemence.

Lew waited until Kenzie had closed the office door behind her. "Doc, did you see what I saw?"

"Kenzie's mask: the old man."

"We should talk with Chip's mother," said Osborne. "See if he said more about what he saw two days ago."

Chapter Eighteen

At ten that morning the sun on the snow across the field was dazzling. And deceptive. Stepping out of the warm kitchen to follow Ray and Bruce off the back deck, Judith reeled back, her cheeks seared by an uncompromising wind out of the north.

Ohmygosh was Ray right about needing something to cover my face, she thought, pulling the fleece neck warmer she had borrowed from Mallory up and over her nose. She had resisted at first, anxious to keep her makeup unblemished. Earlier that morning she had fussed in front of the mirror even though she knew better: Fishing is not a girly sport.

Talk about wasted effort, she thought as she tromped through the snow behind the two men, but looking beautiful is not worth freezing to death.

"Hey, wait for me," came a shout from the side of the house. Kenzie Steidl waved as she ran toward where everyone had gathered in the driveway of Rudd's house. "Sorry I'm late."

"Not to worry," said Ray, "but it's so cold I thought maybe you decided not to join us."

Judith noticed Kenzie was well prepared for the cold: Black insulated boots came almost to her knees, where they met the edges of a heavy sheepskin coat. A red plaid hat with earflaps had been pulled so far down on her forehead that Judith could barely make out her eyes. Like Judith, she wore a neck warmer up to her nose, but hers was reinforced with a rainbow-colored wool knit scarf. Sheepskin-lined mitts covered both her hands.

Ray and Bruce had paused to wait, too. "C'mon, ladies, stand still too long and you'll freeze in place." They were pulling long plastic sleds with blue tarps covering their contents.

"Why aren't we driving out?" asked Kenzie when she reached them. "Warmer that way."

"Nah," said Ray, "that's sissy fishing. We're tough—we can make it across the field easy and fish right off the shore in that little bay. Too many razzbonyas further out. I want quiet water where it's not too deep. Ready, everyone?"

Crossing the field was easy. Rudd had contracted with a neighbor to plow a trail wide enough for cross-country skiing. The trail started behind the house and ran down to the shoreline where it continued parallel to the shore. The good news was the trail made it easy to walk in their heavy boots; the bad news was no protection from the wind.

Turning her back whenever a gust hit so hard that her eyes watered, Judith began to wonder if she had been too eager to give ice fishing a try. "Honestly, Ray, this is brutal," she shouted into the wind.

All she got was a thumbs-up from the well-padded, six-foot-six figure wearing a fish on his head. She shook her head and smiled to herself. *How on earth did I get here?* But she kept going.

At the shoreline, they plunged through snow over a foot deep to where they could walk along a snowmobile trail leading into the bay where Ray wanted to fish. To Judith's relief, they hadn't gone far when a stand of balsams crowding the shoreline sheltered them from the wind.

"This is good," said Ray, pulling his sled to a stop. He had been right about too many fishermen. Peering out across the big lake, Judith saw what seemed like a city of wooden shacks and pickup trucks dotting the ice and clustered as if to keep one another warm. But there was no one in the bay.

"First, we need a fire," said Ray. He yanked the tarp off one of the sleds to expose several lengths of firewood.

"That's not much wood," said Bruce. He glanced back at the distance they had just trekked. "A lot of effort for twenty minutes of fishing."

"No," said Ray, "I'm sending you into the woods over there to see if you can find some more." He looked chagrined after pulling the tarp off the second sled. "Actually, I thought I brought more. Guess I was in too much of a rush. Damn."

"Hold on," said Kenzie, pointing behind them in the direction of the field they had just crossed. "I see a pile of logs over by the trees there—on the left. I'll run over and grab some."

"Yeah," said Ray, looking in that direction, "looks like someone clear-cut a small section. Sure, go see what you can get."

"I'll help," said Judith, anxious to keep moving.

"Wait," said Ray as he bent over the second sled to unload six tip-ups, four folding chairs, a bucket full of minnows, a cooler, a thermos of hot chocolate, another thermos of coffee, five jig poles, and plastic containers of waxies and nightcrawlers.

"What's in the cooler?" asked Judith.

"Sandwiches—peanut butter and liver sausage. Now, you two take this sled with you. That'll make it easy."

The snowmobile trail wound close to the shoreline so the going was easy. Even so, it appeared someone had run a plow up to the woodpile.

"I'm not sure about this," said Kenzie, staring down at the logs. "These look so freshly cut, I'm not sure the wood will burn. But what the heck, let's give it a try."

With that, she and Judith began stacking the split logs onto the sled. As Judith reached for one that was near the bottom of the pile, she was surprised to find what appeared to be a metal pipe right beneath it. She pushed several pieces of wood back, exposing bare ground and another pipe-like object.

"That's odd," said Kenzie. "Looks like someone cut the wood to keep whatever this is covered. I wonder if someone is trying to put in a well? That shouldn't happen—this land belonged to my dad. Well, to Rudd's museum now. It's posted, so no hunting and stuff. Weird."

Minutes later, as they unloaded the sled by the bonfire, which Ray had started, they mentioned what they had found. "Really?" asked Bruce. "That's an odd spot for a well. Maybe it's a sprinkler system."

"That doesn't make sense," said Kenzie. "I'll ask Greg if there's some building going on around here. I know Vern bought a back forty from my father years ago, but that's further down the road and there's already houses on it."

"Hold on while I finish these holes," said Ray, who was hard at work with a gas-powered ice auger. When water had splashed up through the fourth hole, he stepped back and turned to scan the field behind them. "Tell me again what you saw . . ."

Judith repeated the description of what they had uncovered.

"That doesn't make sense," said Ray. "That land isn't cultivated, so it can't be a sprinkler system."

"I wonder if Rudd had the architects out to walk the site for the museum," said Judith. "She didn't tell me she'd gone that far yet. I know the conceptual plans have been drawn but not site development. And in the middle of winter?"

"Ladies, let me get you set with tip-ups, then Bruce and I will take a look," said Ray. "Judith, you ready?" asked Ray, demanding her full attention as he knelt in front of one of the holes in the ice. "This wooden platform here . . . is rigged with this fishing line here . . . and a spring with a red flag on it. Now, watch me . . ." He slipped a shiny silver minnow onto the hook and dropped it through the hole in the ice. "When that red flag pops up—you've got a fish."

"Ohmygod, then what do I do? Yikes."

"You holler at me or Bruce. We'll take care of it." With that, Ray rigged another tip-up for Judith and two for Kenzie. Then he and Bruce headed toward shore to see what it was that had been hidden beneath the woodpile.

Chapter Nineteen

After the two men had moved half a dozen more of the split logs, they uncovered yet another metal pipe stuck in the ground. Ray shook his head and glanced over at Bruce with a question in his eyes. "I have no idea what this could be. Maybe someone planning to build a deer stand?"

"Looks to me like a half-assed attempt at soil testing," said Bruce, kicking at one of the pipes that had been sunk down into the ground. "Just recently my brother-in-law had a crew out to his place to bore down and check out the quality of the sand on his property. The mining team brought in a similar setup. This looks pretty do-it-yourself if you ask me, though I wouldn't blame 'em for trying.

"After all, if you're sitting on good silicone sand—and they recently learned that northern Wisconsin has the best in the country—then it could be worth a lot of money. The oil companies who are fracking for oil in North Dakota are desperate for quality sand."

"So . . . if you had a *field* full of the right kind of sand," said Ray, turning to gaze across the field and back toward the faint outline of Rudd's winged home, "what would that be worth?"

"Millions," said Bruce. "If I want to believe what my brother-in-law said, we're talking serious money. Worth futzing around like this to see if you can get enough of a sample to justify the cost of bringing in a team of experts." Bruce looked across the expanse of snow reaching all the way to the main house. "And if you had a whole field full? Probably build and operate a full-scale mining operation right there."

"So Rudd Tomlinson may have wanted to build her museum on land worth millions?"

"Could be. But who knows how the testing went?"

"I'm more interested in *who* did the testing." Ray's eyes met Bruce's. "That cell phone of yours take okay photos in this cold?"

"Believe so." They paused for a moment to study the bay and the bonfire. "I sure hope that new wood burns okay," said Bruce. "When we finish here, I'd still like you to teach me your jigging technique."

"We'll have time," said Ray, watching as Bruce held his phone out to take a series of photos from different angles. "Hey, how many bars does that phone show—enough to make a call?"

"Looks like it. Want me to call Chief Ferris?"

"We'd better. My instructions were to let her know if I saw anything unusual on the Tomlinson property. Since it didn't occur to me to walk the property lines this far from the house, I'd feel better if she was aware someone has been in the area."

Lew took Bruce's call immediately. After listening to his theory and checking the photos that he had emailed in before they spoke, she said, "Good. Now if you and Ray can ballpark when that testing might have happened that would be very helpful.

"But whatever you, do don't say a word relative to any soil testing to Kenzie or Judith. Sand mining has become a hot potato in this county, and I don't want news like this to get out until we know more. Meanwhile, thanks. This puts a whole new spin on things.

"Gotta go. Tim Tomlinson is due here later for his interview with Doc and myself. It'll be interesting to hear if he knows anything about someone fooling around with soil testing."

As Bruce tucked his phone back into his parka and pulled his mitts on, he said, "She'd like to know if we have any idea when this testing might have taken place."

"I figured as such," said Ray. "While you were talking, I checked the stand of balsams running along here for sign of anyone entering from a nearby logging road, but I didn't see anything.

"I think they came by snowmobile. The lake has been frozen over since early December, so they could have been here any time over the last six weeks or so. I know how deep the snow is out on the lake, so I compared that with the height of the snow on these logs, which is a lot less. Since we haven't had a melt in weeks, I'm guessing the wood to cover the test site was cut within the last three weeks.

"Ray! Ray! I got a fish, hurry!" It was Judith hollering from one of her tip-ups. She was jumping up and down like a kid on Christmas morning.

"Okeydoke, I'm coming, I'm coming," Ray shouted back. He winked at Bruce. "Hope I can get her that excited later tonight."

"Pradt, you are incorrigible," said Bruce, grinning as he shook his head. "You should be ashamed of yourself."

Back at the fire, Ray helped Judith slip her fish from the hook. "This is a decent-sized walleye, Miss Fordham. May I invite you . . . later this evening . . . to my humble abode where . . . I will sauté this beauty . . . in the finest Wisconsin butter? You," he pointed his mitt at her, "deserve only . . . the best for such a prize. May I?"

Judith giggled. "Oh, all right. You'll have to put your address in my GPS, though. I have no idea where you live."

"I can do that," said Ray, slipping another minnow onto her line.

Meanwhile Kenzie, sitting near the fire with a mug of hot chocolate between her mitts, asked, "So what do you guys think about those weird pipes we found?"

"Just something left from years ago," said Ray. "Once upon a time your dad might have wanted to put in a tank to hold minnows or a fish hatchery. Something like that." Kenzie shrugged, satisfied with Ray's answer. She kept both eyes focused on her tip-ups.

"Hey, my turn, Ray," said Bruce before Judith had a chance to quiz Ray further. "You keep bragging you have a secret lure for jiggermen. Better show me before I freeze to death out here."

"All right already," said Ray.

He picked up the ice auger and drilled two new holes in the ice—one for him and one for Bruce. Then he pulled over two of the folding chairs and beckoned for Bruce to sit beside him. Holding a short jigging rod in one hand, he sorted through his tackle box while saying, "Last time I used this, I caught a thirty-one-and-a-half-inch walleye—so be prepared."

He pulled out a lurid green jig and showed it to Bruce. "Here's the secret: This is an eight ounce jig and it *has to be* chartreuse. Not red like every other jabone uses. But *chartreuse*. And . . . you have to have a very sharp tip . . . now you add a one-and-a-half-inch nightcrawler . . . " Ray fished in his tackle box for the plastic container holding his worms. "Then you jig . . . but keep your jig within a couple inches of the bottom . . . like this, see?"

"Ah," said Bruce, "that's why you wanted this shallow bay, huh? I wondered why. And no Vexilar?" he asked, referring to a fish locater that is standard equipment for most ice fishermen. Ray shook his head. "Nope. No need to hook that up. I know who's lurking down below us." He raised his eyebrows as he grinned an evil, happy grin.

"You do that with no gloves?" asked Judith, who had walked over to watch.

"You have to," said Ray. "Can't feel the tug otherwise. Like they say . . . the tug is the drug, doncha know."

"Oh, my fingers would freeze." Judith shivered at the thought.

"Your turn, bud." Ray handed Bruce one of his chartreuse jigs and the container of worms. Bruce got his line ready with jig and nightcrawler. He moved his chair so he could sit over the other hole in the ice. The two men sat jigging in silence, their hands naked in the below-zero weather. Judith, watching, finally asked, "Does that lure you're using have to be chartreuse?"

Ray didn't answer her question.

Instead he said, "These two fishermen were out in their boat one day when they heard a woman screaming. So they rushed across the water to her dock, where she told them that her fluffy little dog had been swimming when 'all of a sudden Tiffy was gone. Eaten by a big fish!' 'How big a fish?' asked one of the fishermen. She held her hands four feet apart. 'This big—I saw it grab my little Tiffy.' 'That's a heck of a big muskie,' said the other fisherman. 'So, lady, what color was your dog?'"

Judith stood with a perplexed look on her face for a long minute, then she laughed. "O-o-kay, I get it."

Bruce, meanwhile, was aware that Ray had told his story without his usual hostage-taking pauses, which meant one thing: He must have sand on his mind. Like Bruce, he was ready to get back to town.

Time, they agreed half an hour later, to stop by a certain office before it closed.

Chapter Twenty

Judith had expected to be out on the ice for at least an hour. But in spite of Bruce's excitement after landing two good-sized walleyes, one right after the other, Ray started loading the gear back onto sleds. "Quitting so soon?" asked Judith, taken aback.

"Hey," said Kenzie, "what's the deal? We've been here less than an hour."

"Had a text from Chief Ferris," said Ray as he folded the canvas chairs and wedged his cooler into one of the sleds. "She needs Bruce and me in town to check on something. Sorry, ladies, but I promise we'll walk on water another time."

"Hope so," said Judith, wondering what had happened while the two men were checking out the woodpile. Ever since they'd walked back to the bonfire, they had seemed jumpy.

Even Ray's manner had changed: less teasing, fewer jokes. Yes, she was sure something had happened, something related to those odd metal pieces stuck in the ground. Hoping that Ray and Bruce's behavior had something to do with why and how her dearest friend had been pushed to her death, she pitched in to help load the sleds.

As the four of them trudged back to the house, Judith asked, "As far as dinner at your place, Ray, are we still on or—"

"Yep."

"Shall I bring Mallory along, too? If Bruce is going to be there . . ."

"Oh, I won't stay long," said Bruce. "I'll eat and run."

"Bring Mallory?" Ray repeated Judith's query with a perturbed look on his face. "Maybe not . . . Not sure if I have enough fish. We'll include her next time."

"Oh, okay," said Judith. She liked the sound of "next time."

Reaching the house, they walked around to the front where Kenzie had parked. Bruce opened the door of a small red sedan and helped her climb into the driver's seat. As she backed out of the driveway, he turned to Ray. "Didn't you say that the car seen parked behind the Grizzly Bear Café right about the time that Rudd Tomlinson was killed was a red sedan?

"Was it a Honda Accord like the one our friend is driving?" He pointed to the red car disappearing down the road toward the Steidls's house.

"Yeah," said Ray, "the guy who saw it didn't know what year, though. But yes, he said it was a red Honda."

"Chief?" Dani poked her head into Lew's office. "I found those records you wanted. They moved the archives down to the court-house basement so it took me awhile. They're kinda hard to read." She handed two files over to Lew. Dani was right. They looked hard to read.

"Oh, and I checked to see if there was anything else on the Tomlinsons or Vern Steidl that year, too. Found one more on Mr. Steidl. Thought you might want to see that one, too."

"Thanks, Dani," said Lew. "How did it go with Charlene? Were you able to help her find more information on her birth mother?"

"I think so. At least I found the right address for the division of Catholic Charities that arranged her adoption. She's checking with them now to see if they have a more accurate record of her birth parents.

"You know, Chief, Charlene has a great job with that mining company. You won't believe how much money she makes."

"I hear you, Dani," said Lew. "When you've finished your internship and have your degree, I'm hoping we can make you a good offer, too. Don't you think that working for the Loon Lake Police might be more interesting than researching sand and rocks?"

When Dani had closed the door behind her, Osborne gave a low chuckle. "Lew, you've already talked her out of running a hair salon . . ."

"She doesn't realize how valuable she is," said Lew, walking over to hand him one of the reports that Dani had delivered. "The day we have all our records scanned and accessible electronically, police work will be much easier. But that day is pretty far off and until then, I have to rely on Dani's talent for searching data on- and offline."

She checked her watch. "Sloane Tomlinson won't be here for another ten minutes. You want to check this? It's the accident report on Caroline Tomlinson's death."

Lew's predecessor, the police chief best known to Loon Lake residents as "the man with no laugh," had worked in the era when law-enforcement personnel were required to type their reports on an old-fashioned typewriter with no "deletes" or "edits" to speed the process. Plus, the man was no typist.

Words crossed out, words typed over, plus messy washes of Wite-Out made for a sloppy, if not confusing-looking page. Added to that was the fact that the "man with no laugh" had been the taciturn type, given to few words—a restraint that carried over into his reports.

Quiet though he was, the late police chief had been a keen observer of human nature. And sympathetic to the pressures of trying to make a living in a small blue-collar town where logging barely paid the bills and the number of professionals making healthy salaries was minimal.

More than once, he could see past bad behavior and deliver a warning rather than a jail term: Domestic disturbances would go unreported if everyone involved calmed down; kids setting off illegal fireworks would be straightened out with a visit to their parents and stern looks; and a young Ray Pradt caught poaching on private water learned the hard way that a prize spinning rod could end up on the wall in the chief's office.

When the "man with no laugh" died, his funeral was well attended. The theory being that Loon Lake residents needed confirmation that their secrets had died with him. And they were right . . . for the most part.

The late chief was never forgiving of those chronically inclined to steal, bully, or otherwise abuse their neighbors. Those behavior patterns he did record and save—often in a note handwritten across the bottom of a typed page.

While Osborne checked one of the files that Dani had located, Lew studied the other. This one covered Philip Tomlinson's report that his boat and outboard motor had been stolen from his dock. Within days the boat was found in the possession of the Tomlinson boy, Tim.

The chief's report went on to mention that Tim had confessed to "being in cahoots with Vern Steidl, the caretaker for the Tomlinson properties." While it was Tim who made sure to leave the boat unlocked, it was Vern who had a buyer for the boat and had promised to split the proceeds with Tim. Once Philip learned his son was one of the culprits, he did not want to press charges. But he did fire Vern.

A handwritten note at the bottom of the page mentioned that Philip had shared with the police the fact that he was also canceling two land deals with Vern—he asked that the police keep an eye on the properties in case Vern retaliated with vandalism. As of the date on the report, it did not appear that any had occurred.

Another report from the same year also involved Vern Steidl, though this one had nothing to do with Philip Tomlinson or any of his properties. The incident reported occurred months later and while it involved a piece of land that had once belonged to the Tomlinsons, it was one of the lots that Vern had had the good fortune to purchase before the boat was stolen.

The night dispatcher had received a phone call late one night from a young mother who alleged that someone was running a "large machine" after midnight and the noise was keeping her children awake. On investigating the source of noise, the officer on duty found Vern Steidl dumping fill into a section of wetland in violation of the Department of Natural Resources statutes protecting "natural wetlands." He was given a warning, but "I suspect he'll do it again," the chief had noted.

"He did, too," said Osborne, looking up as Lew read the report aloud. "I remember hearing about Vern filling in a wetland outside Rhinelander when a big box store was about to be built. The good news for the builder was that the bank had not yet signed off on the purchase of the land from Vern. At the last minute, we had two weeks of rain, and during a final inspection it was discovered there was permanent seepage from a nearby swamp. End of deal. No one felt sorry for Vern on that one.

He continued scanning the other file that Dani had dropped off. "Lew, this is interesting. Remember Tim Tomlinson's comment that his sister, Kenzie, had pushed Caroline down the basement stairs?"

"I certainly do. I've been wondering about that ever since. I haven't wanted to act on it until I saw the report."

"Well, he's flat-out lying. It says here that Officer Roger Adamczak arrived with Pecore right behind the ambulance, and he states that Catherine Schultz, the cleaning lady, said she saw Caroline slip and fall.

"I knew Catherine," added Osborne. "She cleaned for many of the families in town, including Mary Lee before the girls were in their teens. A hard-working woman who raised three kids all on her own."

"So she was at the Tomlinson house when it happened?"

"It says here that she had just washed the floor in the pantry where the door to the basement was located. Caroline came rushing in, wanting to run down to the basement for a suitcase. Apparently she was planning to drive the children down to Lake Forest later that day.

"Catherine told her to wait for the floor to dry, but she went ahead anyway. She slid on the wet linoleum and pitched headfirst down the basement stairs."

Osborne paused to read more. "Catherine was hysterical when Roger got to the house and kept saying it was all her fault. He mentions, too, that the youngest child—that would be Kenzie—was asleep upstairs. No mention of the other two children being around. Lew, you can check this accident report with Roger, but Catherine passed away a few years ago . . . "

"I'll go with Roger's report. If Catherine Schultz was right there and saw it happen, I'm good with that."

"Why would Tim Tomlinson say such a thing?" asked Osborne.

"Because he's a sicko," said Lew. "I can't get those paintings of his out of my head. Frankly, Doc, I expect he'll throw anyone he has to under the bus to get the Tomlinson money. How much you want to bet I'm right?"

A knock on the door to Lew's office and Sloane Tomlinson, wrapped in a thick fur coat with a hood pulled up over her head and carrying a bushel of a purse, bustled in.

"Hello, Chief Ferris, Dr. Osborne. I'm sure I have nothing of importance to tell you, but here I am and I will do my best." Tossing the hood back, she threw the fur coat down onto one of the two chairs in front of Lew's desk and plopped herself into the other one. Osborne picked the coat up, moved it to a chair near the conference table at the far end of the room, and then sat down in the chair beside Sloane.

Lew offered Sloane coffee or a bottle of water, both of which were refused as Sloane made it clear she was short of time. "Let's get this over with," she said, the corners of her mouth spiking down as she spoke.

"Sure," said Lew. "Sloane, I'm under the impression that you didn't care for Rudd. If I'm correct, can you tell me why? Was there something that happened between the two of you?"

"Aside from the fact she stole my inheritance, nothing much happened." Sloane tipped her head up and back as she focused her gaze toward the windows at the far end of the room. "I did not kill her or arrange for someone else to kill her, if that's what you mean." She picked at a piece of lint on her slacks before heaving a sigh. "Isn't that all you need to know?"

"How did you get along with your father?" asked Lew.

Sloane gave her a sharp look. "What does that have to do with the price of pigs?"

"Just answer the question, please."

"My father was a cold, mean man. He didn't like me or my mother or my brother, so we stayed out of each other's way. Don't ask me why. Just the way it was."

"Did he tell you he didn't like you?"

"He didn't have to. Mother did. She said he never wanted children. End of story."

"How about your brother?"

"What about my brother?"

"Do you two get along?"

"Tim is fine. Why go there, anyway? He doesn't even live here."

"How about Tim and Kenzie—are they close?"

Sloane gave a sigh of exasperation. "Look, if you want a complete picture of the dysfunctional Tomlinson family, you'll have to exhume both my parents and ask them. I don't really know why we are the way we are."

Lew was about to ask another question when Osborne made a subtle move with his right hand. It was their mutual signal to wait, not speak, to let the person being interrogated have the next word.

"You know, when we were kids, Kenzie was the one who got all the attention from our father. She's the only one he ever had time for. But don't you dare take Kenzie's word for anything. She takes things way too seriously. Drove my mother nuts."

A smile stole across Sloane's face as she said, "I'll never forget, there was this one day when Tim and I were goofing around. We told Kenzie we were playing hide-and-seek, and when we found her, we tied her up. Tied her to this big tree in the front yard. She lost it. Started screaming bloody murder. She said that we said we were going to cut her up and feed her to the bears—"

"Did you tell her that?" asked Lew.

"Yes, but c'mon, we were kids. Next thing you know, the old man is running up from his place yelling at us. We had to stay in our rooms for two days. Kenzie got ice cream, for God's sake." Sloane snickered at the memory.

"You thought that was funny? Tying her to a tree?" asked Osborne.

Sloane gave him a dry look. "You had to be there. She was damn lucky our mother died when she did, by the way."

"Why's that?"

"Mother hated Greg. She told Kenzie he was 'trailer trash.' That's because after the divorce Greg lived with his mother in a house trailer. He and Kenzie eloped just two weeks after Mom died.

"Your father lived in a trailer," said Osborne.

"Yeah, well, Mother didn't think much of him either."

After Sloane left, Osborne said, "She's charming."

"She's vicious. Oh, I hear footsteps in the hall. Must be Tim. Isn't this fun?" Lew rolled her eyes.

After polite introductions, Osborne sat back down in one of the chairs in front of Lew's desk and gestured for Tim to take the other, which he did. Unlike his older sister, Tim unzipped his loden-green Filson jacket and hung it carefully on the coat rack inside the door. He sat down, crossed one leg over the other, and crossed his arms over his chest.

"You're not married," said Lew, studying the notes in front of her.

"I don't have time for a family. You may remember I'm an artist and an amateur geologist researching the rock formations and coral reefs in Bonaire. I am a very busy man." Tim's right foot pumped and he continued to hold his arms tight against his chest.

"Mr. Tomlinson, I find the paintings that you sent your late stepmother disturbing."

He gave a hollow laugh. "Why on earth? I have started using new imagery in my work and I wanted her to be aware of that. Very emotional, very raw imagery. I am in a 'Francis Bacon phase,' so to speak. Of course, you wouldn't know his work, but he's a very famous British painter."

"I know Francis Bacon the writer," said Lew. "He's famous. I studied him in college."

"Oh," said Tim, taken aback. "Uh, no, I'm talking the painter, British. I don't know the writer." He sounded mollified but only for a moment. Osborne suppressed a smile, pleased that Lew's remark had forced Tim to drop his pretentious attitude.

"The face of the woman in your painting is your stepmother, Rudd."

"Of course it isn't." The foot pumped harder. "What makes you say that?"

"You stuck photos of her in the corners of two of the canvases and the similarities are unmistakable."

He shrugged. "You are overstating the case, Chief Ferris. Let me explain something." He spoke as if he were addressing a two-year-old. "Rudd was planning a museum to showcase two of America's most significant women artists. Assuming Judith does her job, that museum will draw attention from all the serious critics in the country. I was hoping that one of those paintings of mine could be seen—if only in the museum shop. All I want is a *smidgeon* of that attention."

"Well, you've got a smidgeon of my attention, Mr. Tomlinson," said Lew. "Because of those paintings, I consider you 'a person of interest' in the death of Rudd Tomlinson. You are not, under any circumstances, to leave the country. Do you understand?"

Tim said nothing. He stood up and walked back to the coat rack, where he took his time pulling on his jacket. He drew a knit cap from the pocket and pulled it on. He opened the door and paused.

"The 'person of interest,' Chief Ferris, should be my sister, Kenzie. And if you don't believe me, talk to her therapist. She is bipolar, borderline schizophrenic, and capable of causing harm to herself *and* to other people. If you don't follow that up . . . "

"I have," said Lew. "Thank you."

Chapter Twenty-One

Later that day and after Osborne had left to check on Mike, Lew was relieved to find she had a good hour left to catch up on emails as well as the report from Todd Donovan on the alleged accidental drowning of poor young Chip Dietz. After studying Todd's report, she picked up her desk phone and punched in a number.

A woman's voice answered. Soft and shaky. "Yes, who is this?"

"Mrs. Dietz, this is Lewellyn Ferris, Chief of the Loon Lake Police. Do you have a minute?"

"Not really. I'm at the Miller Funeral Home making final arrangements for a memorial for my son. May I call you back?"

"You're only three blocks away from the station," said Lew. "Would you mind coming by here when you're finished? In the meantime, I'll check to see when the Wausau Crime Lab will be releasing your son's remains."

"I would appreciate that," said the woman. "Yes, I'll be by in half an hour, maybe sooner."

Lew got Bruce on his cell and asked him if he'd heard when the autopsy would be completed and the young man's body returned to Loon Lake.

"Should be there in the morning, Chief," said Bruce. "I had a conference call with the guys over lunchtime. They said the pathologist found the kid suffered blunt-force trauma before he hit the water. Whoever did it hit him so hard the skull was fractured in numerous places. The trauma to the brain would have killed him instantly. No water in the lungs. He was dead before he went through the ice."

"Any trace evidence on his clothing or—"

"They're still working on it. That and those cigarette butts that I sent down. Sorry, but this DNA testing takes a while."

"I know, I know," said Lew, sounding frustrated. "Bruce, I know you disagree with me, but I feel like that boss of yours deliberately delays analyses of case materials that belong to this department. You've heard what he thinks of women in law enforcement. He's determined to make me look bad."

"Chief, you're cranky. You need some time on hard water."

"I need sleep," said Lew.

"For the record, the boss is off on his winter vacation. I'm making sure nothing gets delayed."

"Thanks, Bruce. Oops, I have another call—"

"Before you hang up, Chief. Ray and I are over at the Wisconsin Silica Sands office. Ray fishes with Rob Dickerson, one of the mining engineers here, and we asked him to take a look at the photos we shot on the Tomlinson property. You know, the metal pipes that we found drilled under that woodpile?

"Rob's got a real interesting take on these photos. You need to know what we found. Be over in a bit, okay?" He hung up before Lew could say she was expecting someone, someone who might also have critical information.

As it happened, her visitor arrived early.

Donna Dietz was in her mid-fifties but she looked older. A plump woman who wore her brown hair in a simple page around her face, she had chosen a hairstyle that might have been old-fashioned but it highlighted her best feature: large, serious brown eyes. Brown eyes rimmed red at the moment. Lew recognized her immediately.

"You were the librarian at Pike Bay School when my daughter was there." Lew walked around the desk with her hand out.

"That's a few years ago," said Donna. "Yes, I retired six months ago. I remember your daughter. How is she doing?"

Lew offered a quick snapshot of her daughter's career and family—but only a few sentences. She was sensitive to the fact that Donna had just lost her only child. This was not the time to talk of your own child's health and success.

"Oh, he told me exactly what he saw," said Donna once Lew had directed the conversation back to Chip's alleged drowning. "I asked for every detail since Chip and I figured he would have to be a key witness when they, I mean you, caught the guy.

"He said he saw an old man run by the window in the direction of the street just before—like less than a minute before—the truck ran over that poor woman. Old guy with white hair, wearing wire-rimmed glasses."

"He didn't happen to mention if he had a beard or what he was wearing, did he?"

"No beard. I asked about that, too. He didn't notice what the old guy was wearing, Chip said, because he could only see him from the shoulders up. The window over the sinks in the café kitchen is pretty high. One thing, though, that he *wasn't* wearing, and that Chip thought real weird since it was so cold out: *Old guy had no hat on*. No scarf, nothing on his ears like a headband, nothing. And it was thirty-some below zero."

The woman pressed her lips tight together. "I guess that's it. My kid who wants to be a chef gets a good job in a restaurant, happens to look out the window, sees a bad person, and he gets killed. What the hell is fair about that?" The tears welled in Donna's eyes. Lew handed her several Kleenex.

"So am I correct in assuming that Chip might have been able to identify the man if . . . "

"If he was alive, you mean? Yes, Chip was confident he would recognize the man." Donna looked off into the distance. "In fact, he felt good about that. It made him feel important, you know?"

"Was it unusual for your son to go fishing so late in the day?" asked Lew.

"Heavens, no. That was his way of relaxing after being on his feet all day. He loved to ice fish—plus all that free walleye, those bluegills. Do you know how much it would cost if we had to buy our fish in the store?

"I will say this. My son headed out to fish feeling pretty darn good that night. He has a bunch of fishing buddies he runs into out there on the lake. He always liked to stop by a couple of shacks and see what was up. A habit he picked up from his dad when he was alive. They're regular fellows, those guys. They all knew Chip and he knew them. That's why I'm having a luncheon at St. Mary's after the funeral Mass—Chip had lots of friends."

"Would you say that people fishing out there, guys in their shacks, for example, would know to expect Chip to show up on a regular basis?"

"Probably. But I can't imagine that any one of those . . . I mean, most people around here hadn't even heard about the truck accident yet. It wasn't until the six o'clock news that . . . Are you trying to tell me that Chip didn't drown?"

"Donna . . . " Lew got up from her chair and walked over to put an arm around the woman's shoulders. "I heard the autopsy report a little while ago. Your son was murdered. He was dead when his body went into the water. He did not drown."

Donna sat still for a long moment. "Do you think he felt pain?"

"I think, I'm sure, someone hit him from behind and he never knew what happened."

Again Donna was quiet. Then she asked in a soft voice, "When can I have my baby?" Both women wept.

After Donna left the station, Lew walked across the hall to where Dani was working in the conference room. "Didn't you mention that you're on Facebook with Kenzie Steidl?"

"Yes. She friended me a while back. Why?"

"I'd like to check something that she may have posted there. A photo from a recent family gathering that included the victim, Rudd Tomlinson."

"Sure, let's see if we can find it," said Dani, pulling her laptop out of the leather bag that she carried it in. "This will just take a minute," she said, turning it on. "First, let me make sure Kenzie is still on my 'friends' list." Dani's fingers moved fast. "Yep, there she is . . . so we'll go to her page . . . Got it, and it looks like I can access her photos."

Dani scrolled through the photos on the screen until Lew, pointing, said, "That one—the one with everyone wearing masks."

Dani clicked on the photo and it filled the screen. Once again Rudd was standing in the center of the group with a happy expression on her face. "What a friendly-looking person she is," said Dani.

"Was," Lew's tone was grim. "Maybe too friendly. Can you zoom in on that one person?" She indicated the old man with wispy white hair and wire-rimmed glasses. Dani enlarged the photo and Lew leaned forward to study the man's features.

"Chief, you know that's just a mask, right?"

"Yes. Kenzie told me it's hers. Very realistic, isn't it?"

"Too real for me," said Dani. "Reminds me of this mean old man lived next door to us when I was growing up." She shivered at the thought.

Lew continued to study the photo, only now she was interested in the faces of the partygoers caught standing behind the celebrating mask wearers: Who else was there that night?

Kenzie had commented that "I always have to have family" and it appeared this was one of those gatherings. Though their images were in the background, Lew could make out Sloane chatting with Vern and another woman. Maybe a neighbor? Or Vern brought a date? Or a friend of Sloane's?

Although *who*, thought Lew, would want to be friends with Sloane? She chastised herself: That was not a kind thought, but it was honest.

She sat back thinking. "Dani . . . how many red Honda Accords do you see driving around Loon Lake?"

"Serious?" Lew nodded. "A lot. Hondas and Toyotas—you can't get away from 'em. Well, except for Ford 150 trucks. Want me to search the DMV database?"

"Yes, please. I want to find something to help me change my mind." Dani gave her a quizzical look.

Back at her desk, Lew picked up the phone. "Doc, think you can take an hour to do one last interview with me? I'm using a guerrilla tactic this time: surprise. And I need a reliable witness with me."

"Sure, just let me know what you need from me," said Osborne. "Need me to drive in?"

"No, I'll pick you up."

"I'm ready when you are," said Osborne. He hung up and gazed down at his best friend. "I know, boy, I've been gone so often this week that I've neglected you, haven't I?" Mike agreed wholeheartedly, his tail thumping wildly.

Whenever the old man sounded so chagrined, the dog knew what was coming: extra treats and a new bone. He would survive.

Chapter Twenty-Two

When a half hour had passed and Lew had not yet been by to pick him up, Osborne grew concerned. He was on the verge of calling to be sure she didn't want him to drive to town when he saw her cruiser pull into the driveway.

"Sorry to be so late, Doc," she said as he fastened his seat belt. "I forgot that Bruce and Ray were stopping by. They caught me going out the door, which was good. You won't believe what they found over on the western edge of the big field surrounding the Tomlinson property—"

"Gold?" asked Osborne. "Just kidding, Lew, but you sound so excited. Has to be something good."

"Almost as good—sand."

"Come again?"

"Silica sand—maybe. Ray took Bruce, Judith, and Kenzie out to fish that small bay behind the field. He forgot to bring enough firewood, so the two women saw a pile of cut logs on shore and went over to get some. As they were putting some of the logs on the sled they uncovered a couple of pipes sticking out of the ground right beneath the pile.

"Ray and Bruce went to check it out and found two more pipes under the log pile. Bruce thought it looked like someone had been attempting to do soil testing, so they shot a couple photos and stopped by the Wisconsin Silica Sands office, where a buddy of Ray's, one of the mining engineers, works. He said it sure looks to him like someone has been trying to get samples of the sand around there. If the sand at that location fits the profile of the silica sands needed for oil fracking, the property could be worth one heck of a lot of money."

"The Tomlinson property is worth a lot already," said Osborne. "The lake frontage alone is worth at least half a million dollars."

"I know. And Ray knows that, too. But when he and Bruce told the engineer how many acres of land are in that field where the museum is to be built, he said it could be worth millions. Doc, turns out here in the Northwoods we have what is called 'coarse Northern White sand' and it is ideal for fracking. With the oil frackers planning to use ninety-five *billion* pounds of sand just this year, the demand for quality sand is high."

"So the question is: who was in there testing—right?"

"You got it. Both Bruce and Ray say they figure it may have happened within the last three weeks, too.

"Last thing, Doc. Bruce got the autopsy report on the Dietz boy. He died of blunt-force trauma to the left side of his skull. Someone bludgeoned the poor kid to death and shoved him under the ice. If the county didn't have that dive-rescue squad, I'll bet we wouldn't have found his body until spring."

As she spoke, Lew drove down Tomlinson Road, past the elegant wings of Rudd's home, to the driveway in front of the house where Kenzie and Greg Steidl lived.

She glanced at Osborne as she turned off the ignition. "I'm sure someone thought it would be another three months before we knew he hadn't fallen in by accident. Since he was the only witness who might have identified the old man seen running toward the street where Rudd was hit, that's awfully convenient. It's also why I want to see Kenzie today."

"Anything in particular you want me to say or do?"

"Just listen, Doc. Listen and watch."

Though it wasn't yet five o'clock, the sky was darkening. Lights were shining in the windows of the Steidl home. Lew knocked on the front door and they waited.

"Oh, hello, Chief Ferris and Dr. Osborne," said Greg, opening the door with a look of surprise on his face. He was in jeans and a worn red flannel shirt. "Is Kenzie expecting you? She must have forgotten you were coming—she isn't here. But, please, come in out of the cold before we all freeze." He stepped back, holding the door open.

"She isn't expecting us," said Lew. "Doc and I were over at the main house and I thought we'd take a chance on her being here, as I have a few more questions for Kenzie. Is she likely to be home soon?"

Greg checked his watch. "Maybe ten minutes or so. She had a three o'clock appointment with her therapist and that usually lasts an hour. You are welcome to wait. As you can see from the mess on my drafting table I've been working on some drawings."

Lew and Osborne followed him over to the angled drafting table that had been set up in front of south-facing windows. "That doesn't look like an office building," said Osborne as he studied the blueprints spread out across the table.

"Oh no, this is a house I'm designing for an old college friend. He recently bought a lot out on Shepard Lake and asked me to design what will be his summer home. Pretty nice place if I do it right."

"I didn't know that Vern was into building homes these days. I thought he was strictly commercial buildings," said Osborne.

"This is one of my projects," said Greg. "I've been designing houses on the side—trying to build my own business. At least get enough going that I don't need to work for my dad anymore. Nope," he said as he picked up a metal square, "I want out of Steidl Builders before anyone is sued."

Lew's eyes widened. "Mind if I ask what you mean by that?"

Greg looked from Lew to Osborne before saying, "If *you* don't, Chief Ferris, I'm sure Dr. Osborne knows how my dad operates. He's notorious for building on the cheap. He charges for premium materials, then substitutes crap. He cuts every corner he can when a building is going up. I'm sorry, but it's going to catch up with him one of these days. And I don't plan to be there when it does.

"That's why I'm hoping this situation with Rudd's death is resolved soon. Once Kenzie gets her portion of the money left in her father's estate, we'll have enough to be on our own."

"So you're saying your father is a crook . . . " Lew's comment hung in the air.

"I never believed my mother and her friends until I went to work for him myself. That was five years ago. Once I realized what was going on, it was too late. By then, we needed the money, and architecture jobs are difficult to find in the Northwoods, but . . . well, heck, let's talk about happier things.

"Kenzie and I, for example." Greg's voice lifted as he spoke, and he walked away from the drafting table with his arms outstretched. "See all this—the upholstery, the floors, the wall coverings, the furniture? This is all Kenzie's work. Even that quilt hanging on the wall was made by her."

He turned to them with a proud smile. "My wife is an artist with a real talent for interior design. She loves doing it and I love what she does. Our goal is to run our own architecture firm with me designing homes and Kenzie handling the interior design."

"I will say your home is very attractive," said Lew, looking around the living area and toward the kitchen. "The colors, the fabrics. Looks perfect." She nodded in appreciation.

"Hmm. Perfection—that is part of the problem." He dropped his eyes as he pulled out a chair at the dining room table. "With everything so uncertain since Rudd's death, I think it's important you know a few things about Kenzie. She's so . . . so fragile right now."

"She told me that she's been diagnosed bipolar," said Lew.

"Yes, Type II Bipolar is the diagnosis. She's on a mood stabilizer, Depakote. Also Prozac for when things get too out of whack. The drawback to the drugs is that she needs at least ten hours of sleep. And she's a night owl," said Greg with a roll of his eyes. "So mornings here are pretty well shot.

"Except for this morning, when she was up at the crack of dawn to go ice fishing! But she loves Ray Pradt. He's always been good to her." Greg chuckled. "Would you believe she went to bed at seven last night just so she could be with Ray and the folks. Maybe I should be jealous?" He grinned.

"Greg, I got the impression from her brother, Tim, that she has been—"

"Thank you, Tim," said Greg, his grin vanishing. "I am sure he had to mention she's been in psychiatric units over in the cities twice in the last few years. But those were voluntary—and brief—commitments. She and I both felt it was the wise thing to do and that's how we found the Depakote, which has been a lifesaver, believe me."

"She's lucky to have you in her life," said Osborne. "Sounds to me like *you* are the most stable influence."

"Kenzie and I have known each other since we were kids," said Greg. "I know her highs and lows. I know she can be obsessive-compulsive. I know she can be 'certifiable,' but I also know she is gifted. We work together so well. I . . . just . . . I can't stand right now how she is being treated by her family—and my family." He ran his fingers over his head in a gesture of frustration.

"My dad is the worst. The way he talks to her sometimes. And don't get me started on Tim. That's one mean SOB. I'd kill him if I could—but then I would be the one to go to jail." Greg gave a harsh laugh.

"Kenzie told us he abused her years ago," said Lew. "She said that you intervened—"

"Wait," Greg looked stunned. "Are you serious? She told you about that? She won't even discuss that with her therapist. How on earth—"

"She was standing with us in the main house when Judith unpacked a box of horrific paintings Tim had sent to Rudd," said Lew. "She took one look before running off in a panic. Ray caught up with her and brought her back. She was hysterical."

"Oh, my gosh." Greg's eyes moistened. "So that's why she insisted on seeing her therapist today. She didn't tell me. Poor sweetie." Pressing his fingers against his eyelids, Greg took a deep breath.

"Are you okay?" asked Lew.

"I will be. Sorry about this. I just get a little upset at times. I'll be fine." He gave a shaky smile.

"What's with your dad and his rudeness to Kenzie?" asked Osborne.

"It started years ago when she was a kid and he was still the caretaker on the family property. Her mother, Caroline, adored my dad." Greg raised an eyebrow. "*Adored*. Need I say more? One more reason my parents divorced.

"Kenzie was the only one of the three Tomlinson kids who was close to their father. Philip was a kind, quiet man and he was good to Kenzie. Tim and Sloane have always resented that—and my father, too. I would also say," Greg hesitated, thoughtful, "I would also say that Kenzie is the one who most resembles her father physically."

"Tim and Sloane are big-boned, large people," said Osborne.

"They aren't just 'big-boned,'" said Greg. "They're fat. Fat and mean. Like I said earlier, don't get me started on those two. But Kenzie has always been small like her dad. Easy to pick on, which is what her mother did and what Sloane and Tim still do. Unless I'm around. *I do not let that happen.*

"And yet my wife is a kind-hearted person, which makes it easy for people to take advantage of her. Sloane will be rude as hell to her one day, but when Sloane is sick or needs help, Kenzie is there for her. Not so for Tim, though. That damage has been done."

"Don't you wonder how three people from the same family can be so different?" asked Osborne, knowing it was a rhetorical question. An only child himself, he had often wondered what his siblings might have been like if he had had any.

"Kenzie's therapist once told her that every child in a family has different parents," said Greg. "That's been true for the Tomlinsons, for sure. That reminds me—you know that crack my father made the other day and in front of everyone? Accusing Kenzie of not taking her meds?"

"I heard that," said Lew. "Made it sound like your wife is unstable without her medication."

"On the one hand that's true," said Greg, adding, "she does need the meds. But she was behaving like any normal person given the circumstances, so why say that in front of people?"

"Just so you know—a couple weeks earlier Kenzie let Vern have her car for two whole days," said Greg. "Then he goes and makes that nasty crack. God, I cannot wait to get out from under that guy. Sheesh."

"Your father borrowed Kenzie's car? The little red Honda?" asked Lew.

"Yes. He said he was having problems with the brakes on his truck and Kenzie didn't hesitate to let him borrow hers." Greg's face softened. "That's my Kenzie."

The front door opened as he spoke. Carried in on a blast of cold air was a slight figure swathed in a long sheepskin coat, her bright eyes barely visible under a colorful scarf.

Chapter Twenty-Three

"Oh, hey there, Chief Ferris and Dr. Osborne," said Kenzie, looking up as she pulled off her boots. "How come you're here? Don't tell me you found who pushed Rudd in front of that truck?" She stood still, holding her breath.

"No news yet, I'm afraid," said Lew. "I apologize for dropping in like this, but Dr. Osborne and I have a few more questions for you. One has to do with your Halloween party."

"Oh?" Kenzie shrugged off her coat and tossed it onto a chair before joining them at the dining room table. "Whew, it is chilly out there." She blew on her fingers. "What would you like to know?"

"I was hoping you could show us that mask that you were wearing—the old man mask," said Lew.

"Of course," said Kenzie, jumping to her feet, "but why would you want to see that?"

"Has to do with the people attending your party," said Lew, hoping her bluff would work. "Your stepmother was obviously enjoying herself, so I'm checking on a few things including the masks that the people around the table were wearing—and who all was at the party."

"Oh, okay, then you'll want to see that photo again, too," said Kenzie. "Be right back. I have all my Halloween decorations put away downstairs." She jumped up and ran over to a door leading to the basement. Osborne could hear her running down the stairs.

"Kenzie is very organized," said Greg. "Trust me, she'll have that mask for you in a flash."

Sure enough, it could not have been more than three minutes before they heard her running back up the stairs. She appeared in the doorway with a large plastic Rubbermaid bin in her arms. Across the front of the bin was scrawled in black Magic Marker the word "HALLOWEEN." She set the bin on the floor by her chair.

"Alrighty then, let's see what we got here," said Kenzie, lifting the lid. She reached down to pull out two folded sections of black-and-white nylon fabric. "Ghosts," she said with a grin. "I hang them in front of the garage." Next was a white laminated tablecloth covered with black and orange pumpkins. Kenzie leaned over, rifling through paper plates, napkins, and other decorations that filled the bottom of the bin.

"That's odd," she said. "The mask isn't here. That's very odd."

"Maybe you have one more container?" asked Greg.

"No, honey, you know I keep all the Halloween stuff in this one. It sits right next to my Christmas ornaments . . . " She looked puzzled. "Let me think. I know I had it out to clean it."

She grimaced and gave Lew and Osborne an apologetic look as she said, "When you wear that thing it gets kinda slick with saliva around the mouth area. Too much information, I know, but that's why I remember cleaning it real well before putting it away. Otherwise, next year it would be disgusting. I wiped it off with bleach and then I cleaned that off, too."

She glanced off toward the wall, thinking. "I'm pretty sure I tucked it right under the ghosts. Darn. I'll keep looking. Give you a call when I find it?"

"I would appreciate that," said Lew. "Do you mind taking a few more minutes to show us your photo from the party?"

"Oh, sure."

"I'm confused," said Greg while Kenzie was in the kitchen getting her iPad. "Why are you so interested in that mask? Or even the Halloween party? Is there some connection with Rudd's death?"

"The young dishwasher at the Grizzly Bear Café told us he saw an old man run past the café window just before Rudd was hit. Since the driver of the logging truck insists that he saw Rudd pushed from behind, I want to find that old man."

"I still don't see what Kenzie's mask has to do with it."

"His description of the old man is very similar to the mask. Since the boy gave his mother a more detailed description of what he saw, I'd like to show her the mask. It may help us identify the person once we find him."

"Are you also saying that maybe the person who pushed her was wearing a mask?"

Lew hesitated before answering. "Could be," she said. "If Kenzie can buy a mask like that, anyone can. Right?"

"Yes," said Greg. "Because you cannot possibly think that was Kenzie's mask that the dishwasher saw."

"Right now, Greg," said Lew, "I have no idea who might have been wearing such a mask—or even if it was a mask. It's just an odd coincidence that the descriptions match. That's all."

Greg gave a sigh of relief. "The kid ought to be able to tell you, too. Why ask his mother?"

"Because he's dead."

"Wait, you're not talking about that young guy who drowned ice fishing? He's the same person who saw someone who might have pushed Rudd?"

"Yes."

"Whoa . . . " Greg was speechless.

"Greg," Lew lowered her voice, "please, this conversation—especially my interest in the mask—is confidential. Understood?"

"Absolutely." He was still shaking his head when Kenzie walked out of the kitchen with her iPad.

Twenty minutes later, Lew and Osborne thanked Kenzie and Greg for their time. "Sorry I couldn't find that mask for you, Chief Ferris," said Kenzie. "I'll let you know the minute I find it."

"When you do, I want you to call me right away," said Lew. She scribbled her cell phone number on a page from her notebook and handed it to Kenzie. "This is my personal cell and you'll reach me without going through dispatch." Kenzie took the note, folded it, and slipped it into the back pocket of her jeans.

As they dashed for Lew's cruiser, Lew and Osborne tucked their heads down against the wind. "Jeez," said Osborne, "these people live in a wind tunnel." He was reaching to open the car door when Lew motioned for him to walk around the cruiser to where she was standing.

Kenzie had parked her Honda in front of the garage door and alongside the cruiser. "Take a look, Doc," said Lew, pointing down. "Don't you think that rear tire on Kenzie's car looks awful low? Does to me." The floodlight over the garage made the tire easy to see.

"It sure does," said Osborne. "If you promise to warm up the car, I'll run back and let Greg know they should check on it."

At Osborne's knock, Greg opened the front door. "Back so soon? Did you forget something?"

"No, no, just want to let you know that the right rear tire on Kenzie's Honda is quite low. She might have a nail in it. Could be dangerous on these icy roads."

"Thank you. I'll check it right now," said Greg, reaching for the keys to Kenzie's car, which were on a table in the front hall. He pulled on his parka and gloves and followed Osborne out to where Lew was waiting for him.

"You're right," said Greg. "I better pull the car into the garage and get the spare on. Too late to get it in to the tire shop today, I'm afraid. Thanks for catching it."

He climbed into the Honda and hit the garage door button. He pulled the car into the heated garage, happy for once they had opted to heat the garage when they were building the house: It would be no fun changing that tire in the bitter cold. He decided to tackle changing the tire the next morning.

As they started the drive back to town, Osborne could see Lew's face in the glow from the instrument panel. "You look disappointed, Lewellyn."

"Not disappointed. Determined." She kept her eyes on the road. "When Donna and I were talking this afternoon, she mentioned that Chip thought it was odd that the man he saw was not wearing a hat. The neighbor who told Ray about the red Honda parked in front of his house said the car was there a good hour, maybe longer.

"Now who in their right mind with the exception of vain teenage girls doesn't cover their head in this weather? That's why they cancel school. They don't want to risk kids waiting for a bus to get frostbite. Doc, I'm ninety percent sure that if I can find that mask, I will have found at least a connection to the person who pushed Rudd Tomlinson in front of that logging truck."

"You don't really believe that could be Kenzie?" Osborne was taken aback.

"I'm not going to say 'no' yet. Her frustration at not finding the mask among her other Halloween decorations seemed genuine."

"I find her to be so frank and open . . . "

"I do, too. That's why I wanted you with me just now. If she's lying, she's fooled us both."

"And her husband."

"One thing I noticed," said Osborne, "that woman is so well organized—she would have made a great dental assistant."

"And a clean freak," said Lew. "Definitely OCD."

"Lew, it's late and I'm hungry," said Osborne. "We've been so busy these last few days that unless Mallory went to the grocery store, which I doubt, my fridge is empty. How about joining me for a bite at the Loon Lake Pub and Café?"

"I was thinking the same thing," said Lew, "but do you mind if I include Bruce? I know he's staying at the Inn until tomorrow."

"Fine with me."

Bruce answered Lew's call immediately: "I'm glad you called, Chief. I was supposed to go out to Ray's tonight, but I know he's planning to entertain that Judith Fordham, too. Hate to cramp his style, if you know what I mean."

Lew gave a low chuckle. "I do indeed. Meet me and Doc at the Loon Lake Pub and Café in ten minutes."

Chapter Twenty-Four

Mallory had packed up her briefcase and was about to walk out through the foyer when Judith came down the stairs from the second-floor bedrooms.

"Going home to your dad's place again?" she asked. "Why don't you plan to move in here over the weekend? We have a lot to do over these next months, Mallory."

"Sounds good to me," said Mallory. "If you're convinced we can move forward with the plans for the museum—"

"Without a doubt. The sooner you live here, the better, though I know you want your own place."

"I do, but I'm cramping Dad's style, so moving in here for a short time works great."

"Hey," said Judith with an embarrassed grin, "before you leave, tell me if this outfit looks too dressy for having dinner at Ray's. He's cooking the fish that Bruce and I caught today. Isn't that nice of him?"

Mallory raised her eyebrows before answering. "He's cooking your goose," is what she wanted to say. But she pushed that thought back. Instead she gave Judith's outfit the once-over: designer jeans, a ribbed black sweater with a cowl neck, black Sorel boots. "You look good, Judith."

"Thanks," said Judith, swirling around as she reached into a closet for a quilted coat.

"Do you know what you're doing?" Mallory could not resist the question. "I mean, Ray Pradt could not be more inappropriate . . ."

Judith sat down on the nearest chair. "Are you still in love with him, Mallory? You told me you had a fling with him right after your divorce."

"It wasn't much of a fling. And I was not in the best shape emotionally—so that's my excuse. No, I am not in love with Ray, but I have great affection for the guy. I mean, how could I not? But he is not the kind of man I want to spend my life with.

"On the other hand, Judith, much as I like both you and Ray, I don't want to see you hurt."

"Please. I am at least fifteen years older than the guy," said Judith with a wave of her hand. "I am not interested in getting married. This girl just wants to have fun. You know? A little fun." Judith gave Mallory a beseeching look. "Does that sound so awful? As far as our age difference, look at all the guys with women much younger . . ."

"Okay, then," said Mallory. "You'll have fun all right. Just don't complain to me when—"

As Mallory reached for the door to the foyer, Judith interrupted, "You know, inappropriate men are not all bad. I've learned from every one, though there have only been two others. Still . . ."

"I am guilty, too," said Mallory with a laugh. "We're going to get along, I can tell."

"Move in this weekend?"

"You bet."

"Sorry I'm running late," said Ray, welcoming Judith into his trailer. "Had to stop by Happy Hookers and ended up chatting too long."

"WHAT?"

"Don't worry. It's a bait shop. I needed waxies." Judith's heart slowed.

An hour later, after raving over Ray's sautéed walleye and wild-rice casserole, she asked, "Did you ever find out what those weird pipes were? The ones Kenzie and I found under the logs?"

"We did. Bruce and I spent some time with one of the engineers working on the sand mines that are being developed in this area. He agrees with Bruce that someone was doing some soil testing in that vicinity. Did Rudd ever mention that she had been approached by one of the mining companies?"

"No . . . but now that I think of it, I do remember something to do with the land in that area. It was over the holidays. She said that Vern Steidl had asked to buy a strip of land in the field west of her home. He swore Philip had once promised to sell it to him."

"Probably before Vern was fired years ago," said Ray drily. "You heard that story—how he colluded with Tim to steal Philip's fishing boat?"

"No. Are you are kidding me? When was that? Philip didn't share much about his early years with Rudd."

"Gosh, it was back when Tim was a teenager, so that had to be about twenty years ago. So you think Vern approached Rudd on a land purchase recently?"

"She mentioned it in passing when we were sitting in front of the fire one evening. She turned him down and didn't say more about it."

"Excuse me, Judith," said Ray. "If you can wait a moment for my famous lemon-meringue pie, I need to make a quick phone call to Chief Ferris."

Judith listened as Ray apologized for interrupting Lew's evening but he thought she should know that Vern Steidl had shown an interest in the property. "Very interesting," said Lew when he had finished. "Not much I can do about it this evening, but I know how I can follow up in the morning. Go back to your dinner, Ray, and have fun."

"I will." And he did.

Lew put her cell phone away and turned back to Bruce, who had just asked her how to fish a nymph like the Rapunzels he'd seen at Rudd's home. "Bruce," she asked, "have you tried fly-fishing with wet flies?"

"No, only dry flies so far. But I want to learn—"

"The difference is the wet fly needs to sink below the surface of the water. To make that happen, I use a weighted nymph, which will sink to the bottom. Also, you attach a strike indicator to the line so you can check the speed as it moves with the current. When you see the slightest change—you strike!

"Bruce, it's not the easiest technique, but once you get it down, it can be deadly."

"No kidding," Bruce grinned through his moustache. "Sounds fun. Chief, I have another question. Couple guys I know who fly-fish were talking about 'mending' the other day. I know I can look it up, but I thought you could maybe show me how you do it?"

"'Mending' is moving your fly line against the current while you fish your fly, that's all. Maybe they were talking about 'aerial mending,' which is moving your fly line as part of your cast *after* you do the forward power snap that I taught you but *before* your line lands on the water. A simple mend is made with an overhand semicircular move in the upstream direction. Does that make sense?"

"But how wide is the semicircle? Like this?" Leaping up from his chair, Bruce raised his imaginary fly rod and, flinging his right arm back and to the side, managed to knock a tray of water glasses out of the hands of the waitress passing by.

"Oh, jeez, I am so sorry!" Embarrassed, Bruce bent to help the young woman.

When the water had been mopped up and pieces of broken glass disposed of, Bruce sat down at the table.

Before he could open his mouth, Lew said, "Next spring. In the trout stream. Bruce, I promise to take you out on the Prairie River and give you a lesson on mending, aerial mending, and nymph fishing, but only if you sit still right now and finish your meal. No more flailing of body parts."

"You promise, Chief?"

"I do. I'll ask Judith if we can have a couple of those Rapunzels, too. Looked to me like she and Rudd had several dozen that were tied by their instructor."

"I'd like to learn to tie a few myself," said Bruce. "How 'bout you, Doc? Interested in tying some of those trout flies?"

"No," said Osborne. "As a dentist I spent too many years working in small spaces with tiny objects. I will be very happy if you and Lew tie the flies. I'll cast 'em."

Hours later, as they lay in Osborne's bed, Lew tossed and turned, unable to sleep. "Doc," she said after twenty minutes of trying to nod off, "this may sound foolish, but my search for Rudd Tomlinson's killer reminds me of the old saying about a rising fish: *so close yet shy of the surface.*"

"You're convinced the truck driver saw someone push her."

"I've interrogated that guy five times now—and his story has never changed. I just wish he hadn't been so distracted by the sight of Rudd falling that he didn't get a clear view of the killer."

"Any chance you can let go of this long enough to get a good night's sleep, sweetheart?"

"I don't know. But I am happy to be here, Doc. Your place is warmer than mine on blustery nights like this."

He could feel her smile in the dark. "Good." He laid his arm across her and was happy as she snuggled in the curve of their bodies. "I like this. Sleep tight."

"I'll try." Seconds later he heard a light snore. Moonlight, silvery and silent, filled the room. He slept.

Chapter Twenty-Five

Shortly after seven the next morning, Greg finished his third cup of coffee, pulled on his parka, and headed through the door leading down into the garage. Kenzie would be sleeping for hours and wouldn't need the car until later that morning. He had plenty of time to change the tire.

He popped the lid on the trunk and looked down, ready to remove the scrap of carpet covering the chamber where the tire tools were stored. He jumped back.

Staring up at him from hollow eyes behind wire-rimmed glasses were the slack features of an old man.

"Oh, God," he breathed. "Oh, my God." He staggered over to the stairs leading up to the kitchen and sat down. He dropped his head into his hands. "It can't be. Why . . . how . . ." He thought he knew his wife and yet it seemed so obvious that she had to have been the one to push Rudd. But . . . it didn't make sense.

Everything he had heard Kenzie say about her stepmother had been so positive. She had even sounded pleased when her father told her he was planning to marry Rudd—*thrilled* even. Greg thought back through all the years since childhood that he'd known Kenzie.

Yes, he had known her to be manic, depressed, hysterical at times, but that was before the psychiatrist had prescribed the right meds. One thing she had never been was violent. Heck, she was so kindhearted he'd had a difficult time convincing her that mousetraps were a more reasonable solution than live trapping the little stinkers.

Taking a deep breath, he tried to think back over the details of the morning Rudd died. Funny how little he knew about the accident. He checked his watch. He hoped Judith was an early riser. He rushed up the stairs into the kitchen, grabbed his jacket, and shoved the keys to the pickup into his pants pocket.

Before leaving the house, he stopped to check the bedroom. Since Kenzie hadn't gone to sleep until after midnight, he expected her to be zonked out still.

"Hey, honey," he whispered. No response: she was sound asleep. He tiptoed over to the chair near her side of the bed where she had carefully laid her jeans, sweater, and lingerie before climbing into bed the night before. He reached into the back pocket of her jeans. His fingers touched the slip of paper with Chief Ferris's cell phone number. Good. He plucked it from her pocket and crept out of the room.

Judith, still in her bathrobe, opened the door to the foyer with a look of mild surprise. "You're moving early, Greg. What's up? Wait," she held up a cautionary hand, "before you say a word, can I offer you a cup of coffee? I have a full pot brewing. I was out late last night so I'm a little bleary."

"I would appreciate a few minutes of your time if you don't mind, Judith," said Greg as he stomped his feet to knock the snow off his boots.

"Sure," said Judith. "Mallory just got here, too. She's upstairs on a phone call so I've got plenty of time—though I have to get dressed one of these days. Have a seat, Greg."

"Chief Ferris and Dr. Osborne were over late yesterday with questions for Kenzie and me. After they left, I realized I don't know the details of what happened on Tuesday. I'm hoping you can fill in some gaps. Might make my wife feel better."

"Of course. I'm happy to tell you what I know, though it isn't much."

"Thank you. I thought . . . I was hoping you might remember what time the . . . um, accident occurred. Was it early morning? Lunchtime? Maybe early afternoon?"

Judith set a mug of coffee in front of him. "Do you take cream or sugar?"

Greg shook his head no.

She sat down across the table from him. "I know approximately when it happened because I had tried returning a call from Rudd from the road that morning. This was just before nine o'clock. When I couldn't get through after three tries, I assumed that my cell service was spotty so I gave up. In retrospect that must have been right about the time she was hit.

"As far as *officially* hearing about Rudd's death—I got the call from Dr. Osborne just before eleven. Greg, I'm sure Chief Ferris can tell you more."

"I didn't want to call her so early."

"You do know that the driver of the logging truck says that he saw someone push Rudd?"

"Yes," said Greg. "Chief Ferris also told us that the dishwasher at the Grizzly Bear Café said he saw an old man running in the direction of the street."

"That's what I've heard, too. And Ray Pradt was told by a man who lives on the street behind the café that there had been a red sedan parked in front of his house right about that time."

"A red sedan."

"Yes. But that's as much as I know, Greg. Is any of this helpful?"

"Oh, you have no idea," said Greg, pushing back his chair. "Gotta go."

"But you haven't finished your coffee," said Judith, standing up as he ran from the room.

Mallory appeared on the second-floor balcony just as the door closed behind Greg. "What was that all about?"

"I'm not sure," said Judith, taking a sip of coffee and staring at the door Greg had slammed behind him.

Out in his truck, Greg punched a familiar number into his cell phone. "Dad? Are you still home?"

"Yeah . . . " said Vern, his voice thick with sleep. "I'll be in by ten. Had a few too many beers with Tim last night."

"Small emergency here. Kenzie locked her keys in her car with the motor running. We're hoping you might have a spare from when you borrowed her car a few weeks ago."

"Yeah . . . I do. Got it on my key ring right here."

"Great. Be by in a few."

Greg's first impression was relief that Kenzie had not, in one of her OCD moments, informed her father-in-law that they kept a set of spare keys for all their vehicles on a hook by the door leading to the garage. But then, Vern never did pay much attention to anything outside his own world.

Greg punched in the number that Chief Ferris had left. When he heard a woman's voice ask, "Kenzie?" he was thankful to have reached Chief Ferris so quickly.

"No, Chief Ferris," he said. "This is *Greg* Steidl. Sorry to call so early."

"That's okay, Greg," he heard Lew say. "Did you find the mask? Hold on a second, I'm going to pull off the road here while I have good reception."

Phone to his ear, Greg waited for Lew to pull her cruiser to a stop. "Okay, Greg," she said within a few seconds. "Why are you calling? Did you find the mask?"

"Yes," said Greg. "It's in the trunk of Kenzie's Honda, which is in our garage. She's still asleep and isn't likely to wake up until ten at the earliest, maybe eleven. She tends to sleep until noon. I thought you should know."

He waited while Lew didn't answer for a long moment. "This isn't good, Greg."

"I know. But I also know someone who borrowed her car Tuesday morning. Took it while she was sleeping."

"Are you sure?" The police chief's voice tensed. "How can you be sure?"

"I'm not yet. But I'm working on it."

"Don't do that, Greg." Chief Ferris's voice was loud in his ear. She repeated herself: "Please, *do not do that.*"

Greg clicked his phone off and powered it down. He wanted no interruptions.

Seconds later Lew pulled into the parking lot at the station. She ran through the doors. "Who's on patrol right now?" she shouted at the dispatcher.

"Officer Donovan."

"Get him for me ASAP."

Greg let himself through the side door of his father's house, which was on the west side of Loon Lake. Even though his finances had improved over the years, Vern had stayed in the small house he'd bought after marrying Greg's mother. Greg often thought he hadn't cleaned it since, either.

He found Vern, as he had expected, lolling on the sofa in his darkened living room, where he appeared to have slept in a pair of soiled sweatpants and a torn long-sleeved T-shirt. Chatter from a sports channel filled the air.

Over the five years of working for his father, Greg had developed a sense of revulsion every time he saw the man. Initially, he had felt guilty for having such feelings for the man who was responsible for his existence. Not today. Not ever again.

"Dad, you did it, didn't you," he barked. It wasn't a question.

Vern lifted his head from the sofa pillow. "That key is on the kitchen table."

"Forget the goddamn key." Greg marched into the room, picked up the TV remote, and clicked off the television.

Looking down at his father, he said, "You snuck over Tuesday morning and took Kenzie's car, didn't you. You wore that mask and pushed Rudd in front of the truck. Then you killed that poor kid who saw you."

"What the hell are you talking about?" Vern struggled to sit up.

"You know exactly what I'm talking about," said Greg as he started back toward the kitchen. He stopped and turned to face his dad, hands on his hips. "God, you disgust me." He was so angry his voice trembled as he spoke. He knew he had to get out of the house before he strangled the man—or worse.

Vern sat on the edge of the sofa, legs akimbo. "Settle down, will you? I can explain—"

"EXPLAIN!" Greg thought his head would explode.

"Look, there is a way out of all this."

Greg stopped breathing. He could not believe what he was hearing. Vern took his silence as a signal. "See, everyone knows Kenzie is schizophrenic—"

"Who told you *that*?"

"Tim. He knows a doctor who will testify that she was legally insane at the time that she pushed Rudd. She'll have to get psychiatric care for a while, but then they'll let her out. She'll be fine."

"But she didn't push Rudd." Greg tried to sound calm: He wanted to know more.

"We know that, but—"

"But why? Why did you do this?"

"What do you mean '*why*'? Fifty, sixty million dollars is why. That's what that land is worth. Minimum. The field around that house has acres and acres of Northern White sand. Tim said oil frackers are desperate for it."

"So Tim is in on this, too?"

"Well, there was some miscommunication, but it'll work out."

"*Miscommunication?*" As the conversation went on, Greg's nerves steadied.

"Yeah, when we first started thinking about this Tim talked to a lawyer in Bonaire who assured him the lawyer could break the trust so that if Rudd was out of the way, the entire estate—money *and* land—would go to Philip's heirs.

"That means you, son. You and Kenzie will have a fortune. Now you can start that business you keep talking about . . . "

"And some of that will go to you? How?"

"Tim will take care of me. But," Vern shook his head as he stood up, "turns out the lawyer was wrong. You heard from Judith Fordham that only half the estate will go to the family, but that's still a lot of money. All that has to happen now is for Judith to find who pushed her friend."

"So we sacrifice Kenzie."

"I told you. That will work out."

Greg turned around to leave. "Where are you going?" asked Vern as he rolled off the sofa onto his knees. He reached under the sofa.

"I'm not going to let you do this." Greg walked through the kitchen to the side door, his back to the living room.

As Greg opened the door leading out to the driveway where he had left his truck, Vern said, "You forgot something—the key."

Greg turned to answer but no words came out. Astonishment flashed across his face. The blast from the shotgun forced him back against the door.

The Loon Lake Police squad car pulled into the drive seconds after Vern had sped off in his truck. Todd Donovan rushed into the house. He called for an ambulance.

Then he reached Lew: "Looks bad, Chief, but he's alive . . . "

"I'm on my way. Keep him awake. Don't let him—"

"I know." Todd knelt beside Greg. "EMTs'll be here any second, guy. Stay awake. You gotta stay awake—we can't let your blood pressure drop. Please, man, stay with me now."

Chapter Twenty-Six

"Doc, I need help." It was Lew calling on her cell phone from the hospital where Greg was in surgery. Talking fast, she explained what had happened to Greg. "But I haven't had the time to reach Kenzie and I may need help handling her.

"Can you meet me here at the hospital and we'll drive over together? Bruce is going to meet us there, too. I'll give you the details when you get here. Right now I'm standing by to see if they can stop the bleeding."

Osborne caught up with Lew in the ER waiting room and they hurried out to her cruiser. Once they were on the road, Lew said, "I knew after the call from Greg that he was headed either for Tim or for his father. I wasn't sure which, so I directed Todd to Vern's place and I was on my way to Sloane's, where Tim has been staying,"

"Where's Vern now?" asked Osborne. He had been having his last cup of coffee at McDonald's when Lew's call came in on his cell.

"Who the hell knows? He drove off somewhere. I had Roger scout the parking lot for Steidl Construction. He's keeping it under surveillance, but no sign of Vern's truck. He could be hiding in one of the warehouses. I've briefed the sheriff's department, so they're checking those locations."

She pulled into the driveway in front of Greg and Kenzie's house. The garage door was open and the red sedan was parked inside with the trunk wide open.

"If you'll go through the garage and knock on the door to the kitchen, I'll try the front door," said Lew. "Greg said she sleeps very late in the morning, so we may have to wake her."

While Lew was talking, Bruce drove up in his SUV. He got out and walked toward the garage and the open trunk. He looked down, then went back to his car for an evidence bag and nitrile gloves.

Lew banged the brass doorknocker several times but got no response. She walked back around to the open garage door. "Any luck, Doc?"

"No response, but I tried the door and it's open. What do you want to do now?"

"Hold on, let me see what Bruce thinks."

Bruce was holding the mask of the old man in his gloved hands. With care, he turned back the neck section and peered into the mask. "Excellent," he said, eyebrows moving rapidly. "If we're lucky, I'm looking at dried saliva. At least it looks like it to me. Let's hope we got enough for our DNA guys to work with. I'll have this couriered down to the lab ASAP."

"Good," said Lew. "Officer Donovan is at Vern Steidl's place right now and could use your help securing the site."

"Will do."

"Doc," Lew waved to Osborne, "let's go wake Kenzie."

The door to the bedroom was ajar and Osborne could hear the sound of someone stirring as they approached. Lew put out a hand to halt them both. "Kenzie?" she called from the hallway.

"Wha-a—Who's there? Is that you, Sloane?"

"Kenzie, it's me, Chief Ferris. Dr. Osborne is here with me, too. We have to talk to you. Are you dressed?"

The door opened wider and a sleepy-eyed Kenzie, wrapped in a blue chenille bathrobe, her hair askew, blinked at them. "Is something wrong?"

As Lew spoke, Kenzie's eyes widened. "Vern? Vern did this?" Her voice dropped to a whisper as if she didn't risk breathing: "Greg? He isn't . . . is he—"

"No. He is alive, but he is in surgery at St. Mary's Hospital. The doctor is optimistic, Kenzie. So as soon as you can get dressed, we're taking you to the hospital."

"Oh, okay," she said in a weak voice as she sank down into an armchair beside the bed. "Sorry, I'm shaking so bad." She reached for a bottle of pills on the table beside the bed. Her fingers were trembling so violently that she spilled water from the glass on the table as she tried to swallow her medication.

"Should we call your therapist?" asked Osborne. "Would that be a good idea?"

"No, I'll be okay," said Kenzie. "Maybe later, but right now I want to see Greg . . . "

That did not seem like a good idea to Osborne. "Tell you what," he said, "if you'll give me your therapist's name and phone number, I'll give them a call. You're dealing with a great deal of stress, Kenzie. It isn't going to get easier, either." He didn't mention the fury likely to set in once she saw the extent of Greg's wounds.

"All right," said Kenzie. "It's Dr. Sharon O'Hearne and her number is on the wall by the phone in the kitchen."

"Good, I'll take care of that while Chief Ferris helps you get ready."

Moments later, Osborne had the therapist on the phone and he quickly told her that Greg had been shot and was in surgery. "I'll be driving Kenzie to the hospital in a few minutes," said Osborne. "I'm worried about her, though—"

"How's she doing right now?" asked the therapist. "Hysterical?"

"No. But shaken. Very shaken."

"And her husband. Is he going to make it?"

"The doctor thinks so. He's lost a lot a blood and infection is a risk. The good news is the shooter was far enough away that the buckshot was dispersed and did less damage than it might have. No vital organs appear to have been damaged, but the pellets are the problem. The surgeon was still working on him as of half an hour ago. He'll be in surgery for hours . . . "

"Look, Dr. Osborne, I'll meet you and Kenzie at the hospital. Tell Kenzie I'm cancelling the rest of my Friday appointments. I need to be there for her."

"Do you really think that's necessary? I thought maybe a tranquilizer—"

"No. I don't want her taking more medication than she does already. But I also don't want her going into a severe panic attack. That will set her back months and that won't help her poor husband. If I can talk her through these next few hours, she should be able to manage."

After dropping Osborne and Kenzie at the hospital where they were met by her therapist, Lew drove to the station where she asked if dispatch had heard any updates from the sheriff or his deputies.

"Nothing," said Marlaine, who was on that afternoon. "They have an APB out on Vern Steidl's truck, but there have been no sightings. Nothing. They've locked down the area around the construction-company offices, too, in case he were to show up there."

Lew punched in Todd Donovan's cell number. "After securing Vern Steidl's place, Bruce stayed there to complete gathering the evidence and documenting the chain of custody while I drove out to the Tomlinson property," said Todd. "First to Sloane Tomlinson's home. Bruce and I both thought that Vern might try approaching Tim for help, but neither Sloane nor Tim have seen any sign of Vern since yesterday. They're both pretty upset right now. I told them we'd give them an update once we know more.

"Then I drove over to the main house. I'm here right now with Judith Fordham and Mallory. They're planning to go to the hospital if that's okay."

"Not sure about that," said Lew. "Would you put Judith on the phone, please?"

"Yes, Chief Ferris? Judith here. Is Greg going to be okay? And Kenzie? I need to be there for her."

"On one condition, Judith. You must be very, very careful. Vern Steidl is a desperate man and you could be his next target."

Judith was silent.

"Did you hear me?"

"Yes, but staying here isn't going to change that, is it?"

"I want Officer Donovan to stay with you at the hospital until I get there. I have to see someone shortly and in the meantime I don't want you going anywhere, driving anywhere, alone. Am I clear on that?"

"Mallory will be with me—"

"I want Officer Donovan with the two of you until I meet you at the hospital. Now please put him back on the phone and I'll tell him what he needs to do."

"Okay." Judith's voice was so small, she sounded like a terrified child.

"Todd," said Lew, "please drive Judith and Mallory to the hospital and stay with them until I get there. I'm not sure who Vern will go after next. Until we find him, I want Judith in protective custody."

"Got it, Chief."

Lew strode out into the late-afternoon sun. She got into her cruiser and headed in the direction of the Wisconsin Silica Sands office. Checking her watch, she saw it was already three-thirty. She hoped Charlene didn't quit early on Friday afternoons.

Chapter Twenty-Seven

To Lew's relief, Charlene was still at work. The front-desk receptionist called back and Charlene appeared. "Chief Ferris, what a nice surprise." Charlene paused. "You look worried. Is something wrong?"

"Nothing for you to be concerned about," said Lew. "But I could use some information that relates to an investigation that I have underway. I'm hoping you have time to help me out."

"Certainly, I owe you one," said Charlene with a smile. "Come back to my office and we'll see what I can do."

As Lew sat down across the desk from her, Charlene said, "I don't know if Dani told you, but we did locate my birth mother. I've sent a letter to her through the Catholic Charities office that handled my adoption and I hope to hear something back from her soon. But you should know that even if the woman doesn't respond to my letter, it helps so much to have some idea who my birth parents were."

"Good, I was hoping Dani might be able to help you," said Lew.

"So what's up that I might be able to handle for you?"

"I'm trying to locate a person who may have brought a soil sample into your offices for testing. This would be within the last couple of weeks. Is information like that easy to find?"

"Nothing comes into this office that isn't entered into our database," said Charlene, swiveling her chair toward the computer screen mounted on her desk. "We enter all the information: size of samples, locations, and dates. If you can give me an address, I'll see what we've got."

"I'm hoping this works," said Lew as she opened the file holding Rudd Tomlinson's death certificate. She read off Rudd's full name and the home address. "One of my deputies found what looked like tools used to take soil samples on this property. But not a professional effort—kind of makeshift.

"The land is posted, and I'm concerned that someone has been trespassing on private property. I can't be sure the person taking those samples would have brought them here, but—"

"I wouldn't be surprised. You have no idea how many people are checking to see what kind of sand they have," said Charlene. "Honestly, some come in with zip-tops full of sand and dirt." She studied the screen. "I can tell you one thing—our company has not done any sampling in that area. And if we did, the property owner would be notified of our interest and we would submit a legal request for permission before proceeding."

She looked up from the screen. "I see no indication that a request for soil testing came in from a Rudd Tomlinson."

"That doesn't surprise me," said Lew. "Is that the only way you would know if soil on her property has been tested?" She started to get up from the chair. She was anxious to get to the hospital and see how Greg was doing.

"Hold on, Chief Ferris, I'm not finished," said Charlene, gesturing for her to sit back down. "Now I'll search by address. This is similar to reverse phone searches, a process with which I'm sure you're familiar. All samples submitted must include a description and location that the receiving clerk can document in the plat book. If the person was kind enough to give an approximate location . . .

"Yes, here it is. A sample for that location was dropped off ten days ago by a Mr. Vern Steidl on behalf of a client for whom he is planning to build a warehouse—would the client be your party, Rudd Tomlinson? He got the results a week ago today. The sand was rated 'excellent.'"

Charlene looked over at Lew. "Mr. Tomlinson is going to have to make a tough decision: his property is sitting on Northern White sand, which is the best for oil fracking. The clerk made a note here, too, that the property has easy access from the water. Must be near a lake, maybe? That could be a terrific savings, as they could avoid the cost of paying for right-of-way, of cutting a road in, the whole shebang."

"Interesting," said Lew. "You probably can't tell me the value of such a finding."

"No," said Charlene, "not until the owner takes the next step, which is to pay our engineers to survey and test the entire property to see how much sand is there. Quality is only half the equation— *quantity* is the key."

Back at the hospital, Lew waited with Kenzie for Greg to come out from under the anesthesia. Curtains had been pulled around his bed in the ICU. While Lew and Kenzie sat side by side in chairs, a cot had also been brought in for Kenzie to spend the night. Her therapist had gone home after making sure that Kenzie was able to ask Greg's surgeon the right questions. On learning that her husband might be out of the hospital within four days and a full recovery was expected, Kenzie was a new person— efficient, caring, and gracious with the hospital staff.

"No drama," Kenzie had said apologetically when Lew arrived after leaving Charlene's office. "I got myself under control, Chief Ferris."

Next, Lew had arranged for Judith to spend the night or nights, depending on when they were able to apprehend Vern, at the Loon Lake Inn. "I can't have you out at the main house by yourself," Lew had said when Judith tried to argue that she would be fine and four functioning shotguns were housed in the cabinet in what had been Philip's den.

"Absolutely not," Lew had said with an alarmed laugh. "You are staying safe here in town, and Officer Adamczak will be patrolling the Inn's parking lot and hallway around your room through the night."

"This is ridiculous," Judith had argued.

"No, it isn't," said Lew. "Vern Steidl is an angry and vicious man. We can't be sure what he will do next. Rage does not make for rational thought, Judith. Because you may have replaced Rudd in his mind as the person responsible for ruining his life, you could be his next victim, and I refuse to let that happen."

What Lew chose not to add was that she remembered well the rage that had filled her entire being when she learned of her only son's death in a knife fight. If she had been anywhere near the kid who had killed him that night in the parking lot of a beer bar— that kid would have been dead, too. It had taken hours for her to regain her sanity.

Who knew what Vern Steidl was thinking?

Once Judith agreed and resigned herself to a night at the Inn, Lew had sent Osborne and Mallory home. So it was that as it neared midnight, it was just Lew and Kenzie keeping the sleeping Greg company.

His hands moved and Lew stood up. "Call the nurse, Kenzie. Greg may be coming out from under the anesthesia."

Once the nurse had checked his vital signs and Greg's eyelids flickered, Lew asked the nurse, "Is it possible to know if he can hear me?"

The nurse leaned over the bed, grasped one of Greg's hands, and said in a loud voice. "If you can hear me, Greg, will you squeeze my hand?" He did.

"He can hear," said the nurse. "I need to check several things before you talk to him. Greg, can you tell me your date of birth?"

Greg mumbled.

"Good, can you tell me who is our president?"

Again a mumble but the correct answer. After asking several more questions the nurse turned to Lew and Kenzie. "He's doing well. He's alert but very weak."

"Do you think it's okay for me to ask him a few questions— ones he can answer 'yes' or 'no'?"

"I'll check with the doctor on call. He discussed the case with the surgeon before he left tonight. Let's be sure that it's okay before you do anything."

Lew waited. The nurse returned within ten minutes. "If you can communicate so that he doesn't have to talk much, that would be best. I do need to get him to take sips of water, too. So, please, keep it short."

With Greg's right hand in hers, Lew leaned over the bed. "Greg, I need to ask you just three questions. Simple answers are all I need because we can discuss the details when you are feeling better. If you can, please answer 'yes' with one squeeze of my hand or 'no' with two squeezes. Is that okay?" He squeezed her hand once.

"Was it your father, Vern, who shot you?" One squeeze.

"Do you think he knew about the mask?" One squeeze.

"Is it possible he was driving Kenzie's car, the red Accord, this past Tuesday morning?" One squeeze.

"Thank you, Greg. That's all the information I need."

She decided not to add that those three answers from a key witness made it imperative that the Loon Lake Police apprehend Vern Steidl and charge him with murder and attempted murder.

"Chief Ferris," said Kenzie, "Vern would have found that mask easily. If you check our basement, it's well organized. All our bins are clearly marked, like, for Christmas and Halloween. All he had to do was go downstairs when we weren't looking.

"I remember now that he came over last week and wanted to borrow tools from Greg's workshop, so he was down in the basement by himself."

"That helps, Kenzie. Now you get some rest tonight, too. This has been a heck of a day."

Getting to her feet, Lew gave Greg's hand a gentle pat as she let go. "You've been a great help, Greg. Now please get your rest. The surgeon will be here to see you early in the morning. The good news is that he expects you to have a full recovery. And Kenzie will be here with you until you're ready to go home."

Lew turned to Kenzie, who was sitting beside her, tears of happiness brimming in her eyes. "Will you be okay?" she asked the young woman. Kenzie nodded and moved over to take her husband's hand.

It was two in the morning when Lew finished the paperwork that had to be completed before she slept. She checked the APB reports from the sheriff's department and she added to the report of Greg's shooting that had to go out to surrounding law enforcement departments. Most critical was that any police officer or sheriff's deputy sighting Vern be aware that he was "armed and dangerous."

Driving home, all Lew could think of was the comfort of her warm bed. She was exhausted.

Chapter Twenty-Eight

Lew pulled the cruiser through the open doors of the old barn. The farmhouse may not have come with a garage when she'd bought it ten years ago, but the barn worked well, sheltering both the cruiser and her pickup from rain, snow, and wind.

After closing the barn doors behind her, she hurried along the walk she had shoveled from the barn to the front porch of the farmhouse. Clouds obscured any sign of a moon or stars, signaling the approach of a snowstorm.

Should be good sleeping tonight, thought Lew as she entered the screened-in porch. She took off her boots before unlocking the door to the house. Anxious for warmth, she pushed the door open and flicked on a light as she walked into the kitchen.

A rush of cold air surprised her. Dammit, she cursed silently, all that money to convert from a wood burner to a gas furnace and it has to go out on a night like this? Drat.

Oh, well, how cold can it get? I have lots of quilts and it is way too late to drive out to Doc's. Actually, she thought as she looked around the kitchen, it doesn't feel that bad. Maybe I didn't turn the thermostat up high enough. Walking into the living room, she checked the thermostat and turned it up a couple notches. That should do it.

Walking through the living room to the bedroom, she noticed that the bathroom door was half closed, which wouldn't help in keeping that room warm. She pushed it open. Curtains were blowing in front of the window. Had the wind forced the window up? She reminded herself that the rusty latch on the lower sash needed replacing—sooner rather than later from the looks of it.

As Lew moved to shut the window, the shower curtain hanging around the claw-footed porcelain tub was yanked back.

She screamed. Vern Steidl stood in the tub, a revolver in his right hand pointed at her chest. "Shut up, Ferris, and stay right there," he said as he leaned forward to lift one booted foot, then the other, out of the tub.

He motioned with the gun for her to stand back against the sink on the wall behind her. "Move real slow now. Hand me your gun, your cell phone, and your pager. Then keep both hands up where I can see them."

One glimpse of his fervid eyes and Lew did not hesitate to follow orders. The gun was a persuader, too, even if his hand was shaking. She recognized the revolver from her training: a Smith & Wesson .357 Magnum Model 66, known as a Combat Magnum. Those suckers did serious damage.

Without saying a word, she did as she was told: She undid the belt holding the holsters for her gun, the pager, the walkie-talkie, and her cell phone and handed it over. Looking past Vern, she could see where the rush of air had come from: Wind had had nothing to do with it. He had pushed open the bathroom window and crawled in.

Silently Lew cursed the snow bank outside, which was high and hard as a result of snow skidding off the roof. It had been easy for him to get in and she was the numbnut who didn't get around to repairs needed on a hundred-plus-year-old farmhouse. Lesson learned.

As Lew stood still with her hands held high, she hoped her fright at the unexpected sight of a man standing in her bathtub would deceive him into thinking she was truly frightened, frightened in the way most women he knew would be. She wasn't. Not anymore. Now that she had him in *her* sights, she had one goal in mind. And her fatigue had vanished.

Nudging her with his gun, Vern pushed her toward the living room.

"Sit right there and keep those hands up." He backed into the kitchen while keeping his eyes on her. At the door, he gave a quick glance to the right as if he expected someone to be standing out on the porch. He walked back into the living room.

"Go pack whatever you need to keep warm. We're taking a road trip."

"What do you mean?"

"Canada. You are driving me to Canada."

"Why me? Why not just take my car?"

"You and I both know that won't work. But if you're along, they won't stop us. And once we cross the border, I'll be out from under all the bullshit."

"What makes you think you won't be found in Canada?" Vern flinched and Lew could see that was one question too many.

"I have my secrets." Lew wondered if Vern's secrets might include Tim and Quebec. "Now get packing, we leave now."

"My things are in the bedroom . . ." Lew debated how to stall.

"Leave the door open and don't try anything." While Vern watched, Lew rifled quickly through her drawers and reached for a backpack she kept in her closet. "Wait—let me see that." Vern turned the backpack upside down and checked all the side pockets before handing it back to her. "Okay."

"May I ask a question?"

"You can try."

"How did you know where I live?" She was curious. She deliberately kept her home address confidential. Only her colleagues in the Loon Lake Police Department knew where she lived.

"Buddy I hunt with lets me store a couple backhoes in his barn, and he told me a long time ago that you two were neighbors.

All I had to do was walk through the woods between your place and his."

"Oh, so you know Luke Frasier? Seems a nice guy . . . " Lew tried a conversational tone. Maybe that would get Vern to let his guard down.

"He's okay. Hurry up. Got what you need?"

"Yes. But—"

"But *what*? I want to get going."

"The weather. The last weather report had radar showing a major storm moving in before dawn. Snow mixed with rain—the roads will be so icy the DOT was considering closing Highway 51 north of Woodruff. Are you sure you don't want to wait—"

"Goddammit, no. Now out the door." Vern shoved her through the door out onto the porch.

"I'm going, Vern, I'm going. Settle down." She hadn't lied about the weather: The snow had begun falling so hard Lew could hear it land with a soft hissing sound.

Once in the cruiser, Lew moved to turn off her police radio, but Vern grabbed her wrist before she could. "Leave it on. I want to hear when they start following us."

"That won't happen for hours. Not until I don't show up for an early meeting—"

"Leave it, I said." Vern adjusted his position in the passenger seat so he could watch the road and Lew at the same time. She backed the cruiser out of the barn and started down the narrow lane toward the county road.

For the first time in her career in law enforcement, Lew was sorry she had a habit of never leaving the station without a full tank of gas. Once on the highway, her headlights reflected off the snow, which was driving straight at the windshield so that it was impossible to see more than a few feet.

"Put those headlights on dim," said Vern.

"You know which route you want me to take?" asked Lew.

"Yeah, north."

"North up past Hurley or north to Sault Ste. Marie?" Vern was silent.

Apparently he hadn't thought that far ahead. Lew tightened her lips in a grim smile. The colossal incompetence of the man gave her a new appreciation of Greg's contempt for his father, though she did have to give him credit for finding her home and a way in. At least he hadn't broken the window.

"May I make a suggestion?" asked Lew as they neared the intersection where they would have to decide which route to take north.

Vern grunted.

"I think going up through the Upper Peninsula to Sault Ste. Marie will be the fastest—"

"Do it and pick it up, Ferris. You're crawling."

"This heavy snow grabs the tires, Vern—"

"Shut up and drive." Lew raised her eyebrows and kept going.

One hour later, at four A.M., the police radio dispatches grew more frequent with reports of vehicles off the road needing tow trucks. Soon it was announced that schools in the region were closed and all the law enforcement agencies were asking local television and radio stations to encourage residents to stay off the roads.

"Eh, business as usual," said Vern. Just then a large black SUV steamed past them, wet snow spraying up onto the windshield. "See? That driver isn't afraid. Pick it up, Ferris. At the rate you're going, we won't get to the border till Easter."

Lew took a deep breath and pressed down on the accelerator. "Vern, I'm going to brake for a moment to see how icy the road is. Okay?"

He grunted. Lew braked and the tires held fine. "All right, I'll speed up," she said. They hadn't gone five minutes when they passed the black SUV. It had spun out and was on its side in the ditch facing the wrong direction. The driver was standing on the highway waving his arms to flag them down. Vern leaned across Lew to press on the horn. The man on the highway dropped his arms with a shocked look on his face.

"I should radio that in," said Lew.

"No," Vern spat out the word.

"It's very cold and dangerous out there," said Lew. "At least let me give a dispatcher the location of the vehicle."

"I said no." Lew kept her eyes straight on the road. She had one hope and she owed it to the most unlikely person: Officer Roger Adamczak.

Roger was such a slacker that after the third time that Lew discovered he had spent a morning in the Loon Lake Public Library reading Louis L'Amour novels rather than in his squad car patrolling the neighborhoods he'd been assigned, she had been able to persuade the city council to purchase a GPS system for the police department. This would allow the department to check the whereabouts of any of the three squad cars, including Lew's cruiser.

Once he'd learned that Lew could find him anywhere, Roger had shaped up. Her hope this morning was that when she did not show up for her seven A.M. Saturday morning meeting with Dani, someone in the department would remember the GPS tracker and use it to locate her cruiser as she drove north. Who would have ever thought that Dani's simple request to work Saturdays in return for having Mondays off could save my life, thought Lew. But the GPS was so new and had been used only once . . . She refused to think the worst.

The sky was beginning to lighten when Lew could see that the snow had eased and the road had become a black ribbon in front of her. It was six-thirty. By now the police radio was busy with accident reports—but no news of anyone suspecting that one of the region's police officers had been abducted. Lew hoped to hear that bulletin soon.

She glanced over at Vern. He had the revolver braced on his left knee and he was looking straight ahead at the road. As if he sensed her looking at him, he turned to face her with an angry expression.

"Sorry," said Lew, "thought you'd appreciate that the road looks a lot better suddenly."

"I was thinking about that dumb-ass Tim Tomlinson," said Vern. "If it wasn't for him I wouldn't be here. He's the idiot who believed that lawyer when he said if Rudd was out of the way . . . " Vern didn't finish his sentence.

"He was going to pay you, I hope."

"Oh, yeah—half of what he said he'd get. That was a lot of money he was talking about. But, hell, I shoulda known better. That guy can screw anything up. I learned *that* a long time ago."

Lew decided to risk another question. "I . . . um . . . well, since I figure you're not going to leave me alive after this . . . "

"Maybe. Maybe not. Why?" The cocksure expression on his face made her happy she had both hands on the steering wheel so she could resist the urge to punch him out. She chose not to mention that she had no intention of letting Vern get to Canada much less hurt her in any way. How, she didn't know yet, but she had time to figure it out.

"Have you ever killed anyone else?" Lew waited, hoping to hear him confess to killing Chip Dietz.

"Yeah. Years ago a buddy made a pass at my wife, which I didn't appreciate. He had a little hunting accident. You know how that goes," he said with a nasty little grin.

"No one else?" Lew waited but all she heard was a grunt.

Then Vern said, "You seem okay with the fact you might be next. Not afraid to die?"

"Don't know about *fear*," said Lew. "I would prefer not to but I've accomplished much of what I've wanted to do in my life. I'll miss seeing my grandchildren—"

"Hey, the road looks good. Let's see you do sixty—that'll get us somewhere."

Lew checked the road. It looked dry, free of snow for this stretch, anyway. She eased up to fifty. She forced herself to stay calm, to at least *appear* calm, as that seemed to have an effect on Vern, who had relaxed ever so slightly. If only she could get him to let his guard down—all she needed was a moment.

The car was heading up an incline on the highway when it turned sideways and drifted into the oncoming lane.

"Stop!" shouted Vern.

"I can't. Black ice."

The cruiser felt weightless as it flew up and over a snow bank to continue at a steady speed into the woods along the highway. As the trees came at them, branches crashing along the sides of the car, Lew braced for the impact when they would hit a trunk.

She was going to die, but not at the hand of Vern Steidl. That made it easier. Relaxing her muscles, she slumped into her seat, head down as she waited for death.

The windshield shattered. The cruiser stopped.

Vern was quiet. Lew tried her legs, her arms. They worked, nothing seemed broken—or, if it was, she couldn't feel it. She looked over at Vern. The large branch that had smashed the windshield had ripped Vern's head half off. Blood was everywhere.

Lew turned the ignition off and pushed at her side door. It opened a few inches, but she managed to squeeze through. The air was so cold. The snow came up to her hips. She passed out.

Chapter Twenty-Nine

Osborne woke at five A.M. as usual. He hit the button on the radio alarm to hear the news and weather report. Schools closed? Highway 51 closed north of Wausau? Wow.

He picked up the phone to alert Lew. She would have heard the weather report, he knew, but it was a good excuse to call. The sound of her voice, whether sleepy or alert, was always the best way to start his day.

Her landline phone rang and rang. No answer. He tried the cell. Again no answer. That was a first. Even if she was on her way in to the station, she always answered. He called the dispatcher and asked if Lew had arrived.

"Not yet, Dr. Osborne. The sheriff's department tried her pager because of all the road closings, but no answer. Do you want me to have her call you when she gets in?"

"Please," said Osborne. He got up to let Mike out and waited near the door while the dog bounded through the new snow. He didn't like the feeling in the pit of his stomach. What if Lew's cruiser was stuck in that long, narrow driveway of hers? What if the power was down . . . still, the landline phone should have worked.

He called Ray. "You awake?"

"What's wrong?"

"Lew's not answering her phone. I'm worried."

"Time for a road trip?"

"Do you mind? I know it's not even five-thirty . . ."

"Been up for awhile, Doc. The dogs have been restless all night with this storm. Let me fill the thermos and I'll be right over. I got the plow on the truck so we should make it into her place okay."

Ray might have been annoying at times, but, dumb jokes and strange speech patterns aside, he was one of the most reliable people Osborne had ever known. Never would he forget the night that Ray had braved a raging snowstorm to help Osborne get Mary Lee to the emergency room.

Mary Lee, who had never had a kind word for Ray, who had badgered Osborne to make Ray move his house trailer so she didn't have to see it from her windows, who would deliberately turn away if Ray gave a passing, friendly wave when she was gardening in the front yard.

Yet when her bronchitis had turned deadly in the middle of the night, it was Ray who got them to the hospital. And it was Ray who sat silently with his neighbor after the doctor delivered the news that Mary Lee was gone.

As they drove toward Lew's farmhouse, which was on the outskirts of town, Osborne tried both phones again. Still no answer. He checked with the night dispatcher, but no news there either. It was slow going on the highway. The plows may have been out earlier, but the snow was falling so fast and hard that the road was dangerously slick.

Ray turned left onto the narrow lane leading to the farmhouse. Both men could see only the faintest indentation in the snow, which indicated Lew's cruiser must had driven out sometime after it had begun to snow. "Looks to me like she left a while ago. Maybe a couple hours," said Ray.

"That's odd. She worked late last night. I talked to her at eleven and she figured she had another hour of paperwork, maybe two."

Osborne tensed as they neared the barn off to the left of the farmhouse. The doors were open and there was no sign of Lew's cruiser.

"Lights are on in the house, Doc." Ray was running as he spoke. Osborne was right behind him. They rushed onto the porch and into the house. "She never leaves her door unlocked," said Osborne. He ran past the living room into the bedroom where the bed was undisturbed.

At the same time, Ray checked the bathroom. "Hey, Doc, look at this." He pointed to the window next to the toilet, which was open. On the floor under the window were smudges of water and mud that looked like someone had tried to do a hasty clean-up. Without a word, Ray ran back through the kitchen. Once outside, he plunged through the thigh-high snowdrifts around the house to the rear, where he could see footprints someone had left when they'd clambered over the snow bank to the bathroom window.

"Doc," Ray called through the open window.

"Yeah," Osborne answered from inside.

"Call the station. Tell them to call for help. Someone broke into her house from here—"

Before he could finish, Osborne was on his cell. When he called the station this time, the dispatcher listened. "Got it, Dr. Osborne," she said. "I'll get that information out ASAP, but Dani is standing right here and wants to talk to you."

"Put her on," said Osborne. "Dani, I don't have time to talk. Ray and I are on our way back to the station. This is not good—"

"Hold on, Dr. Osborne. You need to know we have GPS on all the squad cars. I'm activating the GPS tracker for Chief Ferris's vehicle right now. Call you as soon as I see where she is."

"Oh, God," said Osborne, turning to Ray. "Dani can trace Lew's cruiser. Please pray she's all right. Oh, dear God . . . "

"Calm down, Doc, and get back in the truck."

"All right. But first, let's turn off the lights." Ray gave him a quizzical look, but he followed orders. They went through the house methodically turning off the lights.

"Feel better now?" asked Ray as they climbed into his truck.

"Lew doesn't like to leave lights on," said Osborne, praying as he spoke that he would have the chance to tell her everything at the house was in order.

Chapter Thirty

Lew woke to the whispers of a strange woman. "Sh-h, don't move," said the voice. "The ambulance will be here any minute. You need to lie still." Leaning over Lew, the woman took her hand.

"I'm Nancy Nickel. My husband, Jim Nickel, and I live right over there." She pointed over her left shoulder. "If your car had gone another fifty feet you would have hit our house. I can't believe you didn't hit more trees. Did you know your car flew forty feet in the air? Jim checked the snow and he could see right where you landed."

"I'm cold," said Lew in a weak voice. She found it difficult to keep her eyes open. She could hear the woman moving, then felt something being laid over her.

"My jacket should help," said the woman. "There—does that feel better?" She placed a warm hand on Lew's forehead and said, "There, there, just relax. Hear the sirens? They're almost here. Black ice all up and down the highway—they said you're the fourth accident in the last half hour. It's been an amazing morning."

Lew took a deep breath and tried to open her eyes. But it was such an effort . . . She heard footsteps as another person approached. "She doing okay, Nancy?"

"I think so. Geez, Jim, don't look at that guy. Too gruesome." She squeezed Lew's shoulder ever so slightly as she said, "I'm afraid your friend . . . Well, he's dead. So sorry . . . "

Over the next hour, Lew felt the haze lift as she was placed on a board, her neck was cuffed, and she was loaded into the ambulance. Quizzed for her name, date of birth, and the name of the current president of the United States, she was able to mumble the correct answers. "You have to call Loon Lake Police," she managed.

"We'll take care of that," said an efficient voice. "Right now we're taking you in for a CT scan. You may have had a concussion and we want to make sure that's all . . . "

"Lew, would you like some ice water?" It was Osborne, and Lew realized two hours had passed since she had been wheeled into a private room.

"How did you get here so fast?" Lew asked as she sipped the water through a straw.

"You went off the road just two hours north of town."

She pushed herself up against the pillows. "It was snowing so hard, I wasn't sure where we were. I know I made it past Florence."

"The roads were so bad, you couldn't go very fast."

"I tried to tell that to Vern—"

"Doesn't matter now. Vern's dead. And you are lucky. The tree limb that went through your windshield got him in the neck and sheared his head halfway off his body. The EMTs said he bled out."

"I got him to admit that he and Tim were conspiring against Rudd but no more than that. Too bad I hit black ice 'cause I had just got him talking."

"Don't worry. Greg got the whole story when he confronted his father. He got Vern to admit that he stole the mask, took Kenzie's car that morning, and pushed Rudd. He's also the person who killed Chip and shoved him under the ice."

"Too bad he's dead. He should be paying for that."

"Lewellyn, count your blessings. Who knows what might have happened to you if he hadn't been killed. You have to make me a promise now."

"What's that?"

"You cheated death twice today. I want you to promise you won't do that again for at least . . . um, six months?"

Osborne knew she was feeling better when she punched him in the arm. "Promise. How soon can I get out of here, and where are my clothes?"

"Over on the chair. When you feel like you can stand up without getting woozy, I can take you home. Once we're at my place, I'll serve you soup and sandwiches and put you to bed. Then I have to wake you every two hours or so to check you. Do you agree to that?"

"C'mon, Doc, is that really necessary?" Osborne gave her the dim eye, and she got the message. "All right then, but can we stop by my place so I can get my robe and a few things?"

"Let me check first. At the moment your farmhouse and the barn are a restricted crime scene. You were abducted, remember?"

"Oh," Lew's shoulders drooped, "that's right. I bet Bruce Peters is out there, too. Poor guy. He's had a heck of a week. Man, do I owe that guy time in the trout stream."

Chapter Thirty-One

One week later Osborne found himself in the midst of a pot-luck dinner party at the Tomlinson main house. In anticipation of spring and the opening of fishing season (or so they alleged), Judith and Mallory had strung ropes of fat little green fish lights around the kitchen, anchoring the strands on the top corners of cabinets. The electricity must have been infectious, as the room buzzed with people.

Ray, in one of Rudd's aprons—bright blue and studded with fish outlined in sequins—was busy over the stove. Butter sizzled in a large frying pan as he flipped fillets of bluegill, which he had dusted with seasoned flour before frying. As each fillet came out, he added it to a white platter already heaped with lightly fried fish.

"Oh, my gosh, I can't stand it," said Kenzie, jumping up and down as she peered over Ray's shoulder. "How soon can we eat?" She was the happiest Osborne had ever seen her. Had to help that Greg was recovering and able to be there without the wheelchair he had been using.

Standing alongside Ray was Mallory, carefully tending a large pot of water. When the water reached the boiling point, she set a buttered strainer filled with wild rice over the water to steam. Osborne knew the next steps well. After all, it was he who had taught her the secret to cooking wild rice.

Now he watched as she covered the strainer with a blue-and-white dishcloth and waited for the steam to pop the grassy kernels.

On the counter beside her was a bowl of sautéed mushrooms, a saltshaker, and a black-pepper grinder, along with more butter—all ready to be tossed with the wild rice. That last step would be his job: He had supplied the rice, Mallory had cooked it, and it was up to Osborne to add the finishing touches to his secret recipe.

Earlier that evening, driving over with his daughter, Osborne had dared to ask Mallory how she felt about Ray and Judith seeing each other almost daily. "I know you and Ray . . . "

"Dad, don't worry about it. Ray and I are friends." She turned to Osborne. "It's odd, maybe, but we're better friends than we ever were lovers. Don't ask me why, but I'm happy with it—and so is he. It'll be interesting to see how serious it gets between those two. Just hope they don't break up before they can help me move."

With an affectionate pat on the knee, Osborne had said, "I am so pleased you got the old Kirsch cabin. It'll be nice to have you close by."

Mallory had smiled. "Almost uncanny how it came on the market right when I was looking for an older place on Loon Lake. It needs a new roof and I'll have to update the plumbing, but it has so much character, Dad. I love it.

"Now that Judith is moving forward on the Tomlinson Museum, I have the job security and the income to enjoy that antique." And she had chuckled with satisfaction.

Osborne didn't say anything, but he was pleased, too. It hadn't been easy, building this camaraderie with his oldest daughter. Maybe it was fighting the same battles with alcohol, paired with their stints in rehab, but they had a friendship now that had not existed when Mallory was growing up.

Or maybe it was as simple as having Mary Lee, with her disparaging comments on just about everything Osborne did or tried to do, now happily ensconced in a heaven designed for neurotic upper-middle-class housewives whose husbands fish too much.

Whatever the reason for their newfound bond, Osborne was determined to keep it close to his heart.

Over at the vegetable sink, Judith was busy washing and drying lettuces for tossed salad. She had already mixed a vinaigrette of olive oil and sherry vinegar with a touch of tarragon. And not to be outdone by any of the other guests, Kenzie and Greg had arrived bearing two homemade pies: wild blueberry ("with berries we picked ourselves," Kenzie bragged) and apple ("from trees Dad and Rudd had planted"). Even Sloane was there, though grudgingly. She had contributed a plate of cheese and crackers. The cheese was a store-brand cheddar. Cheap.

The only person missing at the moment was Chief Lewellyn Ferris. She was working late, as there was to be an arraignment early the next morning of Tim Tomlinson for conspiring with the late Vern Steidl to murder Rudd Tomlinson.

Just as Ray scooped the last bluegill from the frying pan, the door to the foyer opened and Lew bustled in, carrying two six-packs—one of Leinenkugel's Original and another of Sprecher Root Beer. Shrugging off her police parka, she said, "Am I too late?"

"No," everyone said in chorus, "just in time."

Chairs were pulled out and everyone sat down to dinner.

"First, a toast," said Judith, getting to her feet. "To my dear friend, Rudd, without whom so much of the good feeling around this table might not have happened. If only she could be here, too. Cheers."

"Cheers," said all the guests.

When dinner was over and the pies—and ice cream—had been attacked with relish, coffee was served. Again, Judith stood to speak.

"I talked today with the architects for the museum. Over the coming weeks, Mallory and I will be meeting with them and the construction teams so that we can break ground for the museum in early May.

"I want to thank Ray and his friend at Wisconsin Silica Sands, as they were very helpful with the soil testing. The mining engineers tested the fields all around the property and found that the coarse Northern White sand, which is in such demand right now, is limited to a small area close to the shoreline. There is not enough there to make it financially feasible to mine, which is a relief because I love this landscape. Rudd loved it, too. So I am relieved I do not have to decide between building the museum and looking at a mountain of sand. Whew!"

"You have to be the only person in Wisconsin happy *not* to have that sand," said Ray.

"You're right," said Judith. "The other conversation I had this week was with the bank, to return the assets in the Tomlinson estate not needed for the museum to the family. Except . . . Tim." There was silence after that statement.

"What if he's acquitted?" asked Sloane. "He'll need money to pay his defense lawyers."

"You're kidding me, right?" asked Judith.

Osborne was aware that Sloane had been quiet during dinner. She'd responded when spoken to but had not joined the conversations otherwise.

"I doubt he will be acquitted," said Lew. "I was reviewing the police reports this afternoon. Tim Tomlinson and his defense team have an uphill battle ahead.

"Bruce leaned on a good friend of his and we got the DNA reports in late yesterday. Because we were able to get samples from Vern's remains, it did not take long to find matches with the samples on the cigarette butts Ray found by where Kenzie's car had been parked behind the Grizzly Bear Café the morning Rudd was killed, the butts left near the holes in the ice where poor Chip

Dietz had been fishing, and the saliva stains inside the old-man mask. Tough to argue with DNA no matter what Tim thinks.

"And that's only the beginning. Not only will Greg testify to what his father told him about Tim and Vern's collaboration to put the blame on Kenzie, but I will testify that Vern told me he and Tim planned to split the money resulting from the death of Rudd Tomlinson. Tim's lawyers are going to find that I'm a damned good witness for the prosecution."

"To answer your question, Sloane," said Judith, "I wouldn't care if he was acquitted. That could only happen on some technicality. As Chief Ferris just said, we know the bargain he made with Vern. *No money.*

"On a happier note," said Judith, leaning down to take a sip of her wine, "Kenzie, you will be receiving close to twenty million dollars. You'll want to talk with a financial planner and decide how to manage that—"

"No, that has been decided," said Kenzie with a broad smile directed at her husband. "We're using half to start Greg's business. The rest will go to endow a treatment center for teenagers diagnosed bipolar, schizophrenic, or with related mental health issues. I'm already talking with the clinic in Woodruff because I would love for the center to be based there."

"Sloane, what about you? You'll get the same. Do you have plans for your share of your father's estate?" asked Judith.

"I'm moving to La Jolla, California," said Sloane with a smirk. "I am *so* over the Northwoods." She gazed around the table. No one looked upset about that plan. But no one was rude enough to say, "We're so over *you*, too."

Jumping to his feet, Osborne said, "If that's settled, I'm doing the dishes."

"I'm helping," said Lew, reaching to clear plates.

And all were happy with that, too.

Later that night, right after Osborne and Lew had climbed into Lew's double bed ready to snuggle under the quilts, Lew jumped out. "Need to make sure I locked both doors, Doc. Be right back." She ran from the room. On her way back, she checked the bathroom.

"Is the window closed, Lewellyn?" asked Osborne.

"Yes," she said, climbing back into bed beside him.

"Sweetie, do you know how many times you've checked the doors and the window tonight? At least four times. And not a door nor a window has moved since we got home."

"I know. I'll get over it."

Osborne knew that Lew liked to think she was tough. Problem was she forgot she was human. Gathering her into his arms, he said, "Lewellyn, I have a plan."

"You always have a plan, Doc," she kidded. "What is it this time?"

"We—you and I—will spend every night for the next month here at your place. Hope you don't mind if I bring Mike along? He's feeling neglected. Chewed a leg off one of the end tables by my bed this week."

"Of course not, but why? You love your house."

"Yes, I do. But I also know how it feels when someone has violated your home."

Boy, did he ever, remembering as he spoke how the week after a woman had broken into his house and assaulted Mallory that he spent more that month on deadbolts, patio-door locks, and sliding-door security bars than he had all year on fishing lures!

"And you said you've been having bad dreams this week . . . "

He felt her nod against his shoulder.

"Lew." With gentle fingers he pushed the dark curls back from her forehead. "The plan is we sleep here until you feel safe again . . . agreed?"

She answered with a kiss.